The North Plan

by Jason Wells

A SAMUEL FRENCH ACTING EDITION

SAMUEL FRENCH

FOUNDED 1830

SAMUELFRENCH.COM

ISBN 978-0-573-70049-1   Printed in U.S.A.   #20336

MUSIC USE NOTE

Licensees are solely responsible for obtaining formal written permission from copyright owners to use copyrighted music in the performance of this play and are strongly cautioned to do so. If no such permission is obtained by the licensee, then the licensee must use only original music that the licensee owns and controls. Licensees are solely responsible and liable for all music clearances and shall indemnify the copyright owners of the play and their licensing agent, Samuel French, Inc., against any costs, expenses, losses and liabilities arising from the use of music by licensees.

IMPORTANT BILLING AND CREDIT REQUIREMENTS

All producers of *THE NORTH PLAN must* give credit to the Author of the Play in all programs distributed in connection with performances of the Play, and in all instances in which the title of the Play appears for the purposes of advertising, publicizing or otherwise exploiting the Play and/or a production. The name of the Author *must* appear on a separate line on which no other name appears, immediately following the title and *must* appear in size of type not less than fifty percent of the size of the title type.

In addition the following credit *must* be given in all programs and publicity information distributed in association with this piece:

The World Premiere of THE NORTH PLAN was produced by
Portland Center Stage, Portland, Oregon (Chris Coleman, Artistic Director)

THE NORTH PLAN was developed by Steppenwolf Theatre Company, through its New Plays Initiative and was presented as part of its First Look Repertory of New Work at Steppenwolf Theatre Company, Chicago, Illinois;
(Martha Lavey, Artistic Director; David Hawkanson, Executive Director)

The play was subsequently workshopped at
JAW: A Playwrights Festival, produced by Portland Center Stage.

THE NORTH PLAN had its world premiere at Portland Center Stage on January 13, 2012. It was directed by Rose Riordan, and the Production Assistant was Kelsey Daye Lutz. Costume design was by Deborah Trout. The Scenic Designer was Tony Cisek, with lighting design by Colin K. Bills and sound design by Casi Pacilio. The Fight Director was Ted deChatelet. Casting was by Harriet Bass, and the Dialect Coach was Stephanie Gaslin. Jeremy Eisen was the Stage Manager. The cast was as follows:

TANYA SHEPKE.............................Kate Eastwood Norris

SHONDA COX.................................... Ashley Everage

CHIEF SWENSON ....Tim True

CARLTON BERG .... Brian Patrick Monahan

DALE PITTMAN..................................Fredric Lehne

BOB LEE ....Blake DeLong

CHARACTERS

TANYA SHEPKE
SHONDA COX
CHIEF SWENSON
CARLTON BERG
DALE PITTMAN
BOB LEE

SETTING

A police station in a small town in southern Missouri.
In Act I, a back room.
In Act II, the main room.

AUTHOR'S NOTES

The slash (/) indicates the point at which an overlap begins. That is,
the actor with the next line will begin speaking at this point.

To Karen

ACT ONE

(A police station holding area. It contains two holding cells–wire-mesh cages, each about five-feet-square–and a desk. A door, currently open, leads off to the main area of the police station.)

*(***SHONDA COX***, an administrative officer, sits behind the desk, trying to read a pre-law textbook. "Trying," that is, because one of the cells is occupied by* **TANYA SHEPKE***, whose voice we've been listening to since before the lights came up.)*

TANYA. I shouldn't be here if I turned myself in. If I turned myself in, I should be rewarded with a pat on the wrist. I told the dude out front, "I'm hear to report someone driving drunk." He's like, "Who is it?" I'm like, "Me." He's like, "You? Did you have an accident?" I'm like, "No." He's like, "Why are you telling me this?" I'm like, "I'm a good citizen, dude, if I see a crime, I'm obligated to report it and shit, right? By law. And I fucking witnessed *me* driving all the way home drunk out of my fuckin' mind, dude." He's like, "Do you want to sleep it off?" I'm like, "Dude, I fuckin' *slept* it off, this was last night." He's like, "Last *night?* What do you want me to do for you?" I'm like, "I want some credit for reporting a crime and turning myself in, you know? 'Cause that shit was out of control." And he's like, "I'll tell you what. As long as you got home safe and everything, I'm just gonna let you off with a warning. Now don't you…' Oh, he goes, "What's your name?" I go, *"Tanya."* "Now don't you do it again, *Tanya*, I'll let you off with a warning." Like, dismissing me, like I'm fucking feeble or whatever. And I'm like, "Fine. But I turned myself in and that negates the, that clears off the slate, dude."

SHONDA. *(skeptical)* Actually, / that's…

TANYA. Yeah, and he goes, "Are you Catholic?" With like this smirk or whatever, and I go, "What does my fucking religion got to do with it, dude?" Not "fucking," but what does my religion got to do with it, and he goes, "You're thinking of a priest, or whatever. It's not like when you confess in *church*." And I go, "Whatever, dude. *Officer*. I just want to sign something. Anybody calls you up and says, 'Tanya was fuckin', you know, loaded on… I seen her drink six Long Island teas and jump behind the wheel' or whatever, you can just be like, 'Sorry dude, she turned herself in and cleared the slate on that one. She paid her debt.'" He's like, "Who's gonna call?" I'm like, "Officer, I don't know, but I gotta go to work, you know? So could we, you know?" He's like, "What's your name again?" I'm like, fuckin', "*Tanya. Shepke.* Okay?" He goes, "Just a minute," and he goes to the computer or whatever, and I'm standing there waiting for fucking forever, and then he's coming toward me with the fucking handcuffs in his fucking hand. And I'm like "No. Fucking. Way. You cannot fucking do this." He's like, "You have the right to remain…" "Fucking *shit*. I turned myself *in*." "Well, you got some outstanding warrants, Tanya, meh meh meh." You fucking asshole. I was on my way to *work*, goddammit. If I turn myself in, I should be rewarded or whatever. Shit.

Do you know him?

SHONDA. What?

TANYA. Do you know that cop?

SHONDA. We got four people who work here. So yes, I know him.

TANYA. Do you like him?

SHONDA. I don't know him *that* good.

TANYA. 'Cause that's a shitty-ass thing to do, don't you think?

SHONDA. I have no opinion on this. I am just supposed to sit here and / supervise your…welfare.

TANYA. Because thanks to that fuckin' cop, that... douchey ..fuckin' *cop*, no offense... 'Cause / I know...

SHONDA. No offense taken. I'm not a police officer.

TANYA. You're not?

SHONDA. I'm an administrative officer.

TANYA. What's the difference?

SHONDA. I answer the administrative line. I do filing and stuff. I sit in here when we get a female prisoner, which now is the first time.

TANYA. Fuckin' *huh*? I'm the first chick ever got in trouble in Lodus, Missouri?

SHONDA. I've only been here a few months. We don't get many prisoners anyway. Most people just get booked and then they run 'em over to the county facility.

TANYA. Well, then let's fuckin' *go*, man. What the fuck am I doin' here?

SHONDA. We haven't got anybody to take you right now, probably. We got an officer out in the National Guard, with all the stuff goin' on, he might *never* be back. Chief Swenson is always patrolling now, since we been in Threat Level Red...so...

TANYA. *(derisive; she's heard this phrase a lot lately, and it isn't about her)* "Threat Level Red. Threat Level Red."

SHONDA. Yeah. So it's mostly just me and Chris.

TANYA. Who the fuck is Chris?

SHONDA. *(patiently)* The officer. Who booked you.

TANYA. Fuckin' *Chris.* Asshole. Asshole Chris.

SHONDA. Yeah. So we been short-handed with all that's been goin' on. I heard over the radio someone said there was army tanks coming up I-70. They said / there was...some people...

TANYA. That fucker is gonna cost me permanent custody of my kids to my ex-shithead, who's just been waiting for me to go to fucking jail again, which now I fucking *am*, thank you Chris, / you cocksucker Chris.

SHONDA. Ma'am. *Ma'am.*

TANYA. Uh oh. Yes, ma'am? You're / gonna fuckin'…

SHONDA. Can you just keep it down now, for awhile?

TANYA. You're gonna fuckin' "ma'am" me? Mammy? Mammy ma'am me?

SHONDA. *What?*

TANYA. Should I call you Mammy?

SHONDA. I don't wish to speak to you anymore. Do you understand?

TANYA. Oh, you don't wish to? Well, if you don't *wish* to. Sorry. What's your name, then? If you're so offended by nicknames. That are…intended to be jokes. Or… fuck it, just let me the fuck out of here, then. Let me the fuck out of here and you won't have to fucking hear me at all.

I'll call you another name / in a minute.

SHONDA. If you don't be quiet… Now I've been nice to you, I've sit here and listen to you go on, but if you don't shut your mouth, I'm gonna call that officer in here and mace you.

TANYA. Go ahead, bitch, I'm immune to that shit.

SHONDA. *(standing)* Excuse me?

TANYA. Whatever. Sit the fuck down. I'm not interested in talking to you anyway.

I don't know why you need to get all worked up.

Sit down. Nobody's callin' you nothin'.

SHONDA. You got *that* right.

TANYA. *(mocking, but mildly)* "Eh eh *eh* eh."

Whatever. I'm just fuckin' tired.

*(**SHONDA** sits, but warily.)*

Real sympathetic, by the way. You're really so warm the way you sympathize with my problems, while I'm going to jail for trying to do the right thing. Nice. Because my fucking in-laws are gonna have a fucking field day with taking total fucking custody of my kids now. My ex-shithead's dumbass retard of a friend: *Larry Carney.*

La-a-rry Ca-a-rney. Fucker walks in, hasn't said shit
to me in years, "Hey, Tanya, let me buy you a drink,
Tanya. Whatta ya havin', da duh da duh duh." Finally,
I'm leaving, he's like "Don't get another DUI, Tanya."
I'm like "Don't *you* get one, dumbass." I'm halfway
home, I'm like, that fucker's gonna call the cops on
me, that's why he was buying me all them Long Island
teas, get me drunk and testify against me in a court of
law. I took the back roads all the way home, like three
miles an hour, all up on the steering wheel, you know,
staring through the window, the "windshield," stopped
every ten minutes to run around the fucking car, get
some oxygen, what the fuck did *that* look like, do you
think. I woke up this morning, I'm like Larry Carney
is trying to fuck me over for Gene's in-laws, / I mean
Gene's family, *my* in-laws.

(**CARLTON BERG** *and* **CHIEF SWENSON** *are heard from
beyond the doorway. This dialogue is fragmented and
largely indistinct.*)

SWENSON. *(off)* Just come over / here. Stand there.

CARLTON. *(off)* Why don't you acknowledge what I'm
saying? / Can't you see how important this is?

SWENSON. *(off)* Hold on. Chris, take this.

CARLTON. *(off)* Officer:

TANYA. Gene, my / murdering ex-shithead.

SWENSON. *(off)* Hold on. Take it all / straight in there.

CARLTON. *(off)* This is the most important thing anyone
will ever say to you, *ever:*

SWENSON. *(off)* Yeah, I'm listening.

CARLTON. *(off)* You are arresting the one man in this
country who can / prevent the persecution of
thousands of innocent people.

TANYA. He tried to kill me in the bathtub, you know. Gene
did. He / tried to fuckin'…

SWENSON. *(off)* Spell your name.

TANYA. …drown me in the bathtub one time, and I'd be
dead now, except he / fuckin' pussied out.

SWENSON. *(off)* Come on, now.

TANYA. Got me all drunk and held my head under. I saw white fuckin' lights, dude. I saw the fuckin' / tunnel, you know?

CARLTON. *(off)* C-A-R-L-T, while I'm / spelling "Carlton Berg" for you, they're drawing up arrest warrants for half the country.

TANYA. Finally, I just twisted all around till I got my mouth up out of the water and I'm like, / "Please Gene don't fuckin' drown me," and he lets me go.

SWENSON. *(off)* I've heard you tell it plenty of times now.

TANYA. He's all like, / "I can't do it, I can't do it, boo hoo huh huh."

CARLTON. *(off)* And why aren't you listening?

TANYA. I'm like, / "You tried to kill me, you cock." He's like, "I *know.*"

SWENSON. *(off)* It isn't my concern.

CARLTON. *(off)* Not your *concern?*

TANYA. So you know what / he does?

CARLTON. *(off)* Do you know what's happening up at Fort Leonard Wood? / They've got special forces units ready to deploy to St. Louis and Memphis.

TANYA. He takes me to the fucking carnival. I kid you not.

SWENSON. *(off)* I heard all that, / during the longest car ride of my life.

TANYA. He's like, "I'm so sorry, now here's some cotton candy." Whatever. "Now let's go on the…fuckin' / … tilt house thing."

CARLTON. *(off)* You don't know what you're doing.

SWENSON. *(off) (calling)* Hey, Chris.

CARLTON. *(off)* Officer.

TANYA. But I'm the one who / can't have my kids, right?

SWENSON. *(off)* Drop that in the tray, Chris, and go on home.

TANYA. From "All These Legal Problems" which / is like one…

SHONDA. *(to* **TANYA***)* Excuse me.

SWENSON. *(off)* Thanks.

TANYA. One problem all spread / out...

SHONDA. Excuse me.

TANYA. You're / fucking excused.

CARLTON *(off,* Let me make / my phone call.

SHONDA. Can you just be quiet? Please. Something's / going on out there.

SWENSON. *(off)* Can't do it.

TANYA. Oh, that's great, bitch. Fuck you, too.

(**SHONDA** *hovers in the doorway.*)

CARLTON. *(off)* Officer, I'm going to tell you one more time:

SWENSON. *(off)* I'm gonna tell *you* one more time, it's "Chief." And don't do me any favors.

CARLTON. *(off)* I have knowledge of a vast network...

SWENSON. *(off)* What is it, Shonda?

SHONDA. What's going on?

SWENSON. *(off)* Well, we're trying to work that out. Who's in there?

SHONDA. That lady Chris called you about.

TANYA. *(shouting off)* It's a MISTA-A-A-A-KE!

SWENSON. *(off)* You d better keep an eye on her.

TANYA. *(again)* YOU FUCKED U-U-U-UP!

(**SHONDA** *returns, reluctantly, to the desk.*)

CARLTON. *(off)* I have knowledge...

SWENSON. *(off)* Hold on. Sign that for me, Chris.

CARLTON. *(off)* I have knowledge of a vast network / of well-placed criminals...

TANYA. Do I have to lay down on the floor in here?

CARLTON. *(off)* ...who have been plotting the overthrow of the United States / government for weeks, if not months...

SHONDA. If you have to lay down, you do, yes.

CARLTON. *(off)* …even before / the current crisis.

TANYA. I'm wearing my clothes for work. I / have to look presentable, Whatever-your-name-is…

CARLTON. *(off)* Do you understand the significance of that?

TANYA. …for my liveli– My… Don't you have a fucking cot?

SHONDA. No, we do not. Someone / will take you to the county facility shortly.

TANYA. What about a fucking blanket, then? The floor is fucking cold.

(**SHONDA** *gets a couple of blankets.*)

CARLTON. *(off)* I'm asking you again for that phone call.

SWENSON. *(off)* That's up to the feds.

CARLTON. *(off)* It's not up to the feds. It's my right.

SWENSON. *(off)* You know that ain't true.

CARLTON. *(off)* I'm an American citizen.

(**SHONDA** *pushes the blankets through the cage's access slot.*)

TANYA. Fuck / you very much.

SWENSON. *(off)* We'll see what the feds say about that, too. I'll see ya, Chris. Be careful.

(**TANYA** *lays one blanket on the floor, pulls the other one over herself, and lies with her face to the wall. She becomes yet another disembodied voice.*)

(**SHONDA** *hovers at the doorway.*)

CARLTON. *(off)* Okay, maybe it's time to take your job / seriously, Chief? You're on the wrong side of this. Big fan of the feds, huh? You do everything the feds say?

TANYA. I'm just tryin' to explain to you the…circumstances that have brought / me here. All I did was miss one or two court dates.

SHONDA. Can I…?

SWENSON. *(off)* Now you hold on a / second. I've had about enough of you.

(**SHONDA**'s *phone rings.*)

TANYA. I didn't try to kill anybody or somethin', like my ex-dumbshit Gene, / the fuckin...dumbshit machine.

SWENSON. *(off)* I'm gonna put you in holding, and we might could / talk later. Or not.

TANYA. I'm / just tryin' to get some goddamn justice.

SHONDA. *(on phone)* Public Services Police / how may I help you?

SWENSON. *(off)* Get up now. Come over here.

TANYA. I / only missed my court dates 'cause I had to work.

SHONDA. *(on phone)* No, we can't do that. No.

(CARLTON enters, followed by SWENSON.)

CARLTON. This is America, Chief. You can't arrest / people for political crimes.

SHONDA. *(on phone)* Because we're in an emergency protocol.

SWENSON. Is stealing government property a political crime? 'Cause if it is, I can arrest / you for that.

SHONDA. *(on phone)* It means that / we have to concentrate on serious crimes right now.

CARLTON. There *is* no government right now! There's no legitimate government!

SHONDA. *(on phone)* No, / there aren't right now, in Lodus, no, but that...

TANYA. Excuse me, but what in the / fuck is going on?!

SWENSON. *(to CARLTON)* Get in there. *(to TANYA)* Who / are you?

(He locks CARLTON into the other cage.)

SHONDA. *(on phone)* It's / because of the emergency situation.

CARLTON. You have to think about / what you're doing, Chief.

TANYA. Okay, my name is Tanya Shepke, and your boy / Chris out there...

CARLTON. *(to TANYA)* Excuse me, ma'am. / Just one second, okay?

TANYA. …has got me totally trumped on a charge, here, /
    officer.

CARLTON. Excuse me…

TANYA. You're totally excused, now shut the fuck up. *(to
    * SWENSON *)* Officer, can you call Bitter's Tire and Glass,
    and tell 'em I can't come in 'cause I'm sick?

SWENSON. *(to* SHONDA*)* Didn't she get her call?

SHONDA. She used it up already, tellin' somebody "F you."

SWENSON. *(to* TANYA*)* I'll look into your situation.

TANYA. Thank / you, sir.

SHONDA. *(on phone)* It's / not us, it's the *county* that's doing
    it.

CARLTON. What about *my* phone call? Huh, Chief? What /
    about…

SWENSON. Look: You're wearin' me out fast, pal. As far
    as I know we still got a Homeland Security, and they
    want to talk to you about some things. So / you're
    gonna stay right here in my jail until somebody tells
    me different.

SHONDA. *(on phone)* Because we rely on their support. Well,
    / I'm sor–

CARLTON. What am I charged with?

SWENSON. I'm / not entirely sure, at this time.

SHONDA. *(hanging up)* Thank you.

SWENSON. Shonda?

CARLTON. I want my phone call.

SWENSON. Not at this time.

CARLTON. I'm entitled to a phone call.

SWENSON. Not now.

CARLTON. This is like something out of Kafka.

SWENSON. That's right. And you're the cockroach.
    Shonda?

SHONDA. Yes, Chief?

CARLTON. / Chief?

TANYA. Sir?

SWENSON. I'm gonna put a gag on both of you in a minute. I swear I am. You think I don't have 'em? You think I don't have gags here?

TANYA. You don't need to *gag* me, you just need to open your ears. *Sir.*

SWENSON. You can't help yourself, can you?

TANYA. I'm trying to *explain* my / *situ—*

SWENSON. Gag her. Where's the / gag? Where is it?

TANYA. Okay okay okay.

(She hides under the blankets.)

SWENSON. Shonda:

SHONDA. Yes.

SWENSON. Anybody calls about him, you send it to me, okay? You don't say anything about him. Right?

(This is unusual—for both of them.)

SHONDA. Okay.

SWENSON. You don't know anything about him.

SHONDA. All right.

SWENSON. That's how they want it, for now. Up at DHS.

(A beat, while she takes this in.)

SHONDA. Okay.

TANYA. *(a voice from under the blanket)* I'm just trying to make my case known, you understand? This was entrapment. I was entrapped into making a confession that was held against me. This is totally a political crime.

SWENSON. I'll see if we can't get her out of here.

SHONDA. *Thank* you.

CARLTON. *(to SWENSON)* So they don't want you to talk about me. *That's* kinda weird, huh?

(SWENSON exits.)

CARLTON. *(to SHONDA)* I'm sorry, what was your name?

SHONDA. Ms. Cox.

CARLTON. Ms. Cox, do you know what's going on out there?

SHONDA. Well, they're not calling it "martial law." They're calling it a "transitional action," or something?

CARLTON. Okay, I was being *rhetorical.* I *know* what's going on out there. I was asking, like, "Do you know, Ms. Cox, what is going *on* out there," and then, you know, I would make a *point.* About it.

SHONDA. I'm just about fed up with all of y'all today.

CARLTON. You care about civil rights, don't you? You care about individual freedom?

SHONDA. Sir, I'm going to ignore you.

TANYA. *(under the blanket)* Ms. Cox?

SHONDA. Ma'am, don't even start.

TANYA. Ms. Cox…

SHONDA. Don't *start.*

CARLTON. I am in possession of important information. Information that this illegitimate government intends to use against its citizens. They're going to arrest innocent people. I'm only the first. The first of / millions.

TANYA. *(under the blanket) I'm* the first.

CARLTON. *(to* **SHONDA***)* Do you hear what I'm saying?

SHONDA. No, I do not.

CARLTON. I'm saying *millions.* That's not an exaggeration. I have the list.

*(***TANYA*** emerges from the blankets.)*

TANYA. I'm the first innocent, arrested person. You might be the second one, but I'm the fucking first one.

CARLTON. Ms. Cox…

TANYA. Shonda, do you believe that that hoosier could try to murder me, and then take me to the fucking *carnival?* Can you believe that?

CARLTON. They're gonna start rounding people up. Anyone they consider a threat. Protesters, artists, lawyers, journalists, / gun–

TANYA. Fuckin' lawyers.

CARLTON. Gun-owners, / immigr–

TANYA. Fuckin' protesters, for that matter. *Fart.*

CARLTON. Immigrants...

TANYA. *Journalists.*

CARLTON. Um...

TANYA. Fuckin' artists, too. "Artistes." Fart.

CARLTON. It's... Ms. Cox, it's REX 84. Readiness Exercise 1984. You can look it up if you don't believe me.

SHONDA. Look it up where? On the internet?

CARLTON. Yes.

SHONDA. If I can look it up, how is it a secret?

CARLTON. It's happening now, though, is what I'm saying. They're putting this plan into action.

SHONDA. I don't know anything about that.

CARLTON. Well, I'm *telling* you about it.

SHONDA. Well, I don't *want* to know anything about it.

TANYA. Dude, she didn't want to hear my shit, neither, and my husband tried to drown me in the bathtub. I'm / not shitting you.

CARLTON. *(to* SHONDA*)* If you don't get me out of here, a lot of innocent people are going to be persecuted.

SHONDA. Let you *out* of here? How I'm supposed to do that?

CARLTON. Just get the key and open this cage.

TANYA. If you let him out, you better let me out, too.

SHONDA. I'm not lettin' anybody out. You must be crazy.

TANYA. *All* the artists is crazy.

(SHONDA *considers.*)

SHONDA. I mean, I can look up *anything* on the internet. Doesn't mean it's true.

CARLTON. Okay. Sure. But, do you know who I am?

SHONDA. No.

CARLTON. I work for the State Department. The U.S. Department of State. Do you know what that is?

SHONDA. Are you being rhetorical again?

CARLTON. What?

SHONDA. Are you straight-up asking me if I heard of the State Department?

CARLTON. Well, *have* you?

SHONDA. Where do you think you are?

CARLTON. Where do I...? Where do *you* think you are? Because a little while ago I saw a guy roll off an actual turnip truck.

SHONDA. You did not. That's / really rude.

CARLTON. He had a... He had a jug that said, "XXX."

SHONDA. That's stupid.

CARLTON. So forgive me for, you know...

TANYA. That's supposed to be where they keep their moonshine.

CARLTON. What I'm trying to tell you... *Sorry*, okay? For... What I'm trying to tell you is I actually work for the State Department, okay? The *government*. So, this is not just another rumor, you see? I'm an actual... I'm a *reliable source*. I have committed no crime, you understand?

TANYA. Join the club, buddy. They don't care about that here.

CARLTON. It's called Main Core. It's a database of databases. They've profiled the membership of every organization they don't trust. It was part of Ollie North's plan, from back in the eighties, the Continuity of Government Plan, in case of a national emergency. Well, here it is, here's the emergency, and, goddammit, Ms. Cox, they're not just tracking us anymore. They're making the arrests.

SHONDA. Who are they arresting?

TANYA. Me.

CARLTON. The whole list. *Everybody.*

TANYA. And I didn't do shit.

SHONDA. *(to* **CARLTON***)* That does not seem realistic.

CARLTON. Have you turned on the TV lately? Have you been watching all the recent *realism?*

TANYA. TV is bullshit. There ain't nothin' on but the emergency, anyway.

SHONDA. All I know is, maybe everybody needs to calm down is all.

CARLTON. Oh, okay. Hey, on another topic, do you belong to any organizations? Donate money to anything, or… No?

SHONDA. I don't know why you're bothering me with this.

CARLTON. Because I have that database. We have to get Main Core out there. You and I. You want to help people, don't you? Ms. Cox? You want to fight back, don't you?

SHONDA. Fight who?

CARLTON. Fight *who?* The provisional government! These criminals who have taken over Washington!

SHONDA. Those people are trying to restore order to the, to the country after what happened.

CARLTON. *Oh!* Naïve, much?! Shit! *(to himself)* Why didn't I drive north? I could have gone *north! (to* **SHONDA***)* They're not restoring anything! They don't want anything restored! They've just taken over, that's all! They're arresting people. They're censoring the media. The army is surrounding major cities. You don't see a problem here?

TANYA. Same shit, though, / different day, right?

SHONDA. It's been ten days, sir, okay? I'm *not* naïve, but I'm not gonna lose my head and start lettin' people out of jail and runnin' around startin' revolutions because of ten days of an emergency situation.

CARLTON. But I have the Enemies List. I have the names. They've put the North Plan into effect. Not kinda sort of, but for real. People need to know. They need to be warned.

SHONDA. Sir…

CARLTON. Stop! I'm not just some guy trying to catch you up in his crazy theories. I am… I stand before you, a high-ranking m– Okay, more of a, sorry, a *mid-level*, to be perfectly honest, a mid-level member of the State Department and I'm telling you, if you've been wondering what those camps are going up outside your cities, I have the names of the people who will soon be living in them!

TANYA. That's what *I've* been trying to fuckin' say, man, all this fuckin' time. I've been railroaded into fuckin' jail, here, man, by a bunch of moonshine-drinkin' fuckin' hoosiers. Amen to that.

CARLTON. *(despairing again)* Oh, my God. What have I done? Why am I trying to save this ignorant fucking country?

TANYA. Exactly. Fuck this country. Let's wipe the slate clean, you know? Start with some all-new shit. We had our laughs, but it ain't funny no more. This country don't give a shit for me, I'll tell you that. Are you really with the government or were you just shittin' her about that? Seriously. Are you? 'Cause when you do the new money, here's who you should put on it: Skynyrd.
I'm serious, dude. 'Cause the Founding Motherfuckers can kiss my ass.

SHONDA. *(to CARLTON)* Where's the list?

CARLTON. I can't tell you that.

SHONDA. Then how am I supposed to help you?

CARLTON. Just let me go. I know who to give it to. I have a friend.

TANYA. That seems unlikely, just kidding.

SHONDA. There's no way I'm gonna just let you go. So why don't you just give us the list?

CARLTON. How can I give it to you if I'm in here?

SHONDA. Why not just tell the Chief where it is, and let him look it over?

CARLTON. And he just hands it over to DHS, right? Because, I'll tell you, I don't think the Chief is on my side.

SHONDA. But you think I might be.

CARLTON. I think I've got a better chance, yeah.

SHONDA. Why?

CARLTON. Because you're a poor black woman.

SHONDA. What?!

CARLTON. Oh, was I not supposed to notice? Which part, the color of your skin or the minimum-wage civil servant job?

SHONDA. You think you can predict my behavior / because of the color of my skin?

CARLTON. Apparently not, because I predicted you wouldn't be so complacent about / a bunch of greedy assholes taking over your country.

TANYA. Hey, man, don't start bringing race into this. What / do you do for a living? Smartass.

SHONDA. Well, I'm black enough to try to give you a chance to hand over that thing before it's too late.

TANYA. Probably work in a bank, or some shit.

CARLTON. A bank? Five seconds ago, / I said...

TANYA. Bank of America. Fuckin' mortgage department.

(SWENSON *enters.*)

SWENSON. How's it going back here?

TANYA. Chief, I've been waiting / patiently for some...

SWENSON. Hold on a second.

TANYA. For some response / to my concerns.

SWENSON. Hold on. One at a time. Mr. / Berg... M–

TANYA. Whatever. I'm tryin' to keep my kids.

SWENSON. *(to* TANYA*)* Where are your kids?

TANYA. With Gene and that...f-in'...Stacy, b-word.

SWENSON. All right.

/ Mr....

TANYA. "Bitch."

SWENSON. One at a time, okay? Mr. Berg, I wanted to let you know that DHS is sending some agents to pick you up.

CARLTON. I want to go to court first. I want to see a judge.

SWENSON. They don't want that.

CARLTON. I want to go into the system. I have a right to be put in the system.

SWENSON. The feds have requested that we not do that.

CARLTON. There are no "feds." There has to be something "federal" in order to have "feds." They're just a gang of thugs.

SWENSON. You're talking to a Marine, Mr. Berg.

CARLTON. So?

SWENSON. So, if this was a gang of thugs, as you say, I don't believe they'd have the backing of the military.

CARLTON. But they *don't*, Chief. They *don't* have that backing. Not completely. Did you hear about General Hernandez? Of course not, because the news channels aren't allowed to carry it, and on the internet it's just one more unsubstantiated rumor. But I'm telling you it's a *fact* that Hernandez was arrested for not committing his command to the siege on Washington. He's disappeared, Chief. He can't be found in the *system*. Right now, as we speak, an American Army division and an American *Marine* division are facing each other from opposite ends of Pennsylvania Avenue. Nobody wants to fire the first shot, Chief. But that standoff isn't gonna last forever.

SWENSON. Which side are the Marines on?

CARLTON. They're on my side, Chief.

SWENSON. Is that a fact?

CARLTON. Honestly, I don't know. It's an extremely confusing situation. Please let me talk to a circuit judge. They're going to make me disappear.

SWENSON. I'll call 'em back, and tell 'em what you say.

TANYA. / Excuse me.

CARLTON. Who? DHS?

SWENSON. That's who I been dealin' with.

TANYA. / Hello-o-o.

CARLTON. Call 'em back and tell 'em what I *say?* How is that a plan? How do you foresee that working out?

SWENSON. Give me a little credit, why don't you?

CARLTON. Why?! Because of our years on the *road* together? Because of your familiarity with the works of Kafka?

SWENSON. That'd be a start. Also, you don't have any choice. Plus, if you're so much smarter than the rest of us, how come you act like I can't hear you yellin' at Shonda in here?

TANYA. He ain't / smarter than the rest of us. He just thinks he is.

SWENSON. You know, I'm just sittin' right out there. Tell you the truth, I'm glad you don't work for the government anymore, 'cause you can't keep a secret worth a damn. Is it in that laptop of yours?

CARLTON. What.

SWENSON. That Enemy List thing.

CARLTON. No. That would be kind of obvious, wouldn't it?

SWENSON. I don't know where else you could put millions of names, except a computer.

CARLTON. I never said I had it with me.

SWENSON. Okay. Well, those agents'll be here before long. I expect they'll care more than I do. Shonda?

SHONDA. Yes, Chief?

SWENSON. Don't let him go, now.

SHONDA. I was never / gonna let him go.

SWENSON. I'm just teasing you. You need anything?

SHONDA. Do I have to stay back here?

SWENSON. Yeah.

TANYA. Excuse me!

(SWENSON *exits.*)

TANYA. *(cont.)* Excuse me excuse me excuse me!

Did you hear him say "one at a time" and then fucking ignore me? Like I'm invisible. Asshole!

(SWENSON appears in the doorway.)

There you are. Listen, sir, do you remember saying "one at a time"?

(SWENSON closes the door. It is as the closing of a tomb.)

(pause)

TANYA. Sittin' in here, while Gene and Stacy teach my kids to hate me, like I'm a monster.

CARLTON. Shonda.

SHONDA. I'm going to read this book now, all right?

CARLTON. What is it, Pre-Law?

SHONDA. I'm just going to read it.

CARLTON. Because, don't bother. Because in a few weeks those books will all be rewritten.

SHONDA. I heard all this before. I remember when people were Nazis if they wanted health care.

CARLTON. This is different. Did you hear what I said about those soldiers in Washington? That's a real thing, Shonda.

SHONDA. I'm not looking at you. I'm not listening to you. I don't even hear nothin'.

TANYA. Hey, man, *what's* your name?

CARLTON. Carlton.

TANYA. "Carlton." Douchey name. No offense. But I wanted to ask you, if my joint custody situation is contingent on not getting a DUI, and then I get a DUI and miss a court date but then the father is found to be, you know, equally guilt-ridden with his joint custody agreement, does that even up the board, like, wipe the slate clean, you know?

CARLTON. Who do you think I am?

TANYA. Well, I *think* you're Carlton McFuckbag Douchyname, aren't you? But as long as we're in here, I thought we could shoot the shit. So sorry, dickweed.

CARLTON. Have you not surmised from the preceding conversation that I have some problems of my own?

TANYA. We all have problems, dude. I'm in fucking *jail* right now, for example. How about you?

CARLTON. Well, let me see now, *yes*, it appears I'm also in jail. Hm. And I'll probably be sent to a secret prison somewhere in eastern Europe and never be seen again.

TANYA. Oh, Mr. Big Shot. Big fuckin' deal. Good / riddance.

SHONDA. I need the both of you to be quiet now.

TANYA. I have the right to talk if I wish. I have the right to remain silent, and I have the right not to remain silent.

SHONDA. I'm telling you to remain silent.

TANYA. I have the right to remain silent, don't I?

SHONDA. I just *told* you to remain silent.

TANYA. If you *make* me remain silent, then it's not a *right* anymore, is it? It's a *requirement*. It's only a *right* if I also have the right *not* to do it. So if you *make* me remain silent, you take away my right *not* to remain silent. And you and me and everyone knows I got the right to remain silent. So I can talk all I want. What do you got to say to that shit?

*(**SHONDA** storms out, leaving the door open.)*

Fuckin' right. I guess so.

CARLTON. That was actually kind of awesome.

TANYA. Don't try to kiss my ass now.

CARLTON. Look... *What's* your name?

TANYA. Tanya.

CARLTON. Tanya, we don't have much time. You've got to listen to me. You heard my situation, right?

TANYA. More or less.

CARLTON. If you get out of here before I do, you've got to get that information.

TANYA. What information?

CARLTON. Main Core. The Main Core database. It's on a flash-drive.

TANYA. *What*, now?

CARLTON. Oh, my God. Did you not hear *any* of that?

TANYA. Yes, I fuckin' heard it. You stole some Russian Marine shit or something and then you just whine like a baby until all I think about is how you should shut the fuck up. Right? *Got* it.

CARLTON. Look, she's gonna be back any second. We have to figure out how to communicate with each other when she's not looking. We have to come up with some kind of code.

TANYA. They already have that, stupid. It's called "sign language."

CARLTON. You know sign language?

TANYA. Why would I know fucking sign language?

CARLTON. Then why w– ? Never mind. We just need to employ a simple alphanumeric substitution system.

TANYA. Exactly.

CARLTON. Right. A is one, B is two, and so on.

TANYA. Right. Just hold up twenty fingers for Z, genius.

CARLTON. You know the binary system?

TANYA. *(noncommittal)* The binary sitsm.

CARLTON. You must remember the binary system from school: Zeros and ones. On-off. Up-down. Right? *(raises his right hand)* So, first position is ones, that's your pinky. Up is one, down is zero. Second position is twos, middle finger is fours, then eights, thumb is sixteens. So, if you wanted to say "Hi," you'd go "H," *(raises index finger)* "I." *(adds pinky)* See? So twenty-*six*, Z, would be sixteen, *(thumb)* Plus eight, *(adds index finger)* Plus two. *(adds ring finger)* Get it?

TANYA. Yeah, that's perfect. What letter is this?

(She shows him her middle finger.)

CARLTON. *(tolerantly)* "D."

TANYA. *(shows it again)* What about this?

CARLTON. "D."

TANYA. *(again)* What about this?

CARLTON. "D."

TANYA. *(again)* What / about this?

CARLTON. All right! Never mind! What was I *thinking?!* I must have been out of my mind to pin the future of this nation on some meth-addled hayseed! You could have done something with your…

*(**SWENSON** appears in the doorway.)*

/…miserable, your miserable…fucking…!

(He's weeping now.)

SWENSON. Hey. Hey. Hey. You're gonna keep it down in here, or I'm gonna put you both in restraints. We're out here right now tryin' to figure out what to do with you. I'll / put you both down a dark hole if I have to.

TANYA. I didn't say a goddamn thing, officer.

SWENSON. Quiet. And I've had enough of the language, too. We're gonna keep a civil tongue in our heads from here on out. Is that understood?

*(**SWENSON** exits.)*

TANYA. *(a little softer now)* What is the matter with you, Carlton? You're kind of acting like a girl. And I ain't on meth. I don't do meth, you hear? *(testing)* Can you hear me, Chief? Hey, Chief? Hey, I found some weed in here, man. This is some weed. "Fuck." "Shit." "Fuck." He can't hear us right now.
Are you listening to me, crybaby? All I'm sayin' is all that time you wasted with the fuckin' math-fingers, you coulda just told me where the Russian Marine thing is.

CARLTON. It's in my laptop.

TANYA. The computer information thing is on your *computer?* You must be the best secret agent of them all.

CARLTON. No, it's *inside* of it. I took it apart and stuck it in there, under the motherboard.

TANYA. Okay. So where is the laptop?

CARLTON. In that locked room out there.

TANYA. What the fuck, dude?

CARLTON. I know. That's why I need that Shonda to get it. She's got to do it before those DHS guys get here, or it's too late. If I can't make her do it, *you've* got to make her do it.

TANYA. How am *I* supposed to make her do it?

CARLTON. Do you see why I wanted to talk to you with the math fingers? Because we've got a lot to cover here. They're gonna come back in here any minute and you still don't understand the first thing about this situation!

TANYA. Take it easy. I get it. The new government guys want to put the reporters and stuff in prison.

CARLTON. And I have the list.

TANYA. Okay. Let me see it.

(A beat, wherein CARLTON marvels at her density.)

CARLTON. The thing that I put in the computer is the list. The Enemies List. That's what you need to get.

TANYA. Great. What do I do with it?

CARLTON. This is very important. I really need you to listen to this part.

TANYA. Don't talk to me like I'm a fuckin' baby, dude.

CARLTON. You can't give it to just anyone in the media. Not the way things are now. So I'm just going to give you one name of someone I trust. We can keep it simple that way. You only have to remember the one name.

TANYA. Let's *have* it.

CARLTON. There's a man in Houston. He's a writer. Here is his name.

TANYA. Yeah, let's *go.*

CARLTON. His name is: Eldard Mandrishevil.

TANYA. Are you fucking kidding me? To keep it "simple," that's / the guy you fucking picked?

CARLTON. Just write it down. As soon as you get out of here, write it down.

TANYA. Write *what* down?

CARLTON. Eldard Mandrishevil.

TANYA. Exactly! What the fuck is that?

CARLTON. Please. You've got to stay *with* me, here.

TANYA. I'll just put it on the internet.

CARLTON. That won't be enough. It's a huge upload. They'll shut it down in minutes. You're going to need help. This guy can help you.

TANYA. What guy?

CARLTON. Eldard Mandrishevil!

TANYA. I told you that guy's no good. I thought you were gonna come up with a different guy.

CARLTON. When was I...? We haven't got *time* for this. He's a journalist, he works in Houston, look him up. But first, we've got to get my laptop out of that room. So when you get out of here, call Shonda on that phone, and explain to her that the future of American democracy is in her hands. Tell her that the, that the... blood...of millions oh my God, this is hopeless. I just don't see this happening.

(Again, he's lost the will to continue.)

TANYA. You know what would probably appeal to her?

CARLTON. No.

TANYA. Moolah. How much moolah you got?

CARLTON. She's not going to do it for moolah. Anyway, I don't have enough moolah. My moolah has been frozen.

TANYA. Well, how the fuck you gonna pay *me?*

CARLTON. I can't pay you. *What?* I'm trying to get you to help me save this country.

TANYA. Oh, dude. I now realize, for the first time, that you're completely insane. Did you think that I was gonna do this for free?!

CARLTON. Tanya. I don't have any m– *(and yet)* How much do you want?

TANYA. I'm not greedy. I'll take whatever this kind of thing normally pays.

CARLTON. Ten thousand dollars?

TANYA. Are you shittin' me?

CARLTON. No.

TANYA. Fuck yeah, then, you got a partner.

CARLTON. Fine. Tell Eldard that we agreed to pay you ten thousand dollars. Okay?

TANYA. How do I know he ain't gonna stiff me?

CARLTON. He's an honorable man.

TANYA. 'Cause he's givin' me the money first, or he ain't gettin' flashity-fuck.

CARLTON. I'm sure he'll understand that. Now, do you know who you're going to see in Houston?

TANYA. Yes.

CARLTON. Who?

(a beat)

TANYA. Eldard.

CARLTON. You know what? Good enough. Eldard the writer in Houston. You find him and he'll pay you. Now: what are you going to do as soon as you get out of here?

TANYA. I'm 'onna call that black bitch and tell her to get on with the fuckin' revolution, man.

CARLTON. Now, let's just say, maybe, it doesn't work. Okay? Let's say she won't go for it. What then?

TANYA. I can try and talk to that Chief of Police, but I don't think that's goin' anywhere, frankly.

CARLTON. No, I agree with you. I don't think it's going anywhere either. So what do you do?

TANYA. I'm not talkin' to that asshole Chris. "What the fuck are you, a fuckin' Catholic? Hee hee hee." Asshole.

CARLTON. No. I'll tell you what: If nothing else works, you've got to take the law into your own hands, Tanya. This might seem like a funny question to ask somebody in southern Missouri, but do you, by any chance, have access to firearms?

TANYA. What the fuck are you sayin', dude?

CARLTON. I'm saying you've got to get that laptop out of there at any cost. At any cost. Even if you have to take it at gunpoint. You understand?

TANYA. You must be fuckin' looney-tunes. I wouldn't get five miles down the road if I held up a fuckin' police station. They'd have a fuckin' police dragnet on me so fast.

CARLTON. Unless you didn't leave any witnesses.

(*pause*)

TANYA. I'm gonna sit down now, Carlton. You're giving me a chill.

CARLTON. You see why it's necessary, don't you?

TANYA. Deal's off, man. Okay?

CARLTON. We're at war now, Tanya. The rules have changed.

(**SHONDA** *enters.*)

SHONDA. Ms. Shepke: Your bond will be coming through any moment now, and then you will be released on your own recognizance. Okay?

TANYA. Thank you.

CARLTON. Shonda.

SHONDA. I'm supposed to tell you not to talk to me.

(*She picks up her book and reads.*)

CARLTON. Shonda, I can show you documentation that will support every claim I'm making. You just need to let me make some phone calls.

(*Getting no response, he begins gesturing to* **TANYA**, *who also ignores him.*)

CARLTON. *(cont.)* Tanya!

(She shows him both middle fingers.)

(to **SHONDA***)* Goddammit, call 713-362-3575. When DHS gets here, it'll be too late. Just call that number and ask them why you should let me go.

SHONDA. *(quietly, not looking up)* I can't.

CARLTON. Why not?

SHONDA. They'll arrest me for treason.

CARLTON. Not if we stop them. If we can just get the word out, we can all put an end to this.

SHONDA. That seems like too big an "if."

CARLTON. Could you call the Chief back in here, please?

SHONDA. They told him to isolate you if you didn't stop talking.

(He waves again at **TANYA***. When he has her attention, he makes a series of distinct gestures: He points at* **TANYA***. Makes the sign for "money." Points out to the main office. Slashes a finger across his throat. Points at* **SHONDA***. Slashes a finger across his throat. Points again at* **TANYA***. Holds her gaze.* **TANYA** *makes a decision.)*

TANYA. I want more money.

SHONDA. What?

TANYA. *(to* **CARLTON***)* I want more money if I'm gonna help you.

CARLTON. *(covering)* I don't know what you're talking about.

SHONDA. Are you paying her money to help you?

CARLTON. No. I don't know what she's saying. She's on meth, or something.

TANYA. *(to* **SHONDA***)* I can help him if I want, can't I? Make / a phone c–

SHONDA. No, you cannot. Do you want to be kept in here, too?

TANYA. You can't keep me in here for trying to help him.

SHONDA. Can't you understand that these are not normal circumstances?

TANYA. If he wants me to make a phone call or something…

SHONDA. Pay attention. *Pay attention.* They have declared martial law. If you tell people that you are going to help him, then they will not let you go. They will send you wherever they're sending *him*. Do you understand what I'm saying?

TANYA. Well, that's fucked up.

SHONDA. *Yes.*

TANYA. I want a lawyer.

SHONDA. You / want a lawyer for what?

CARLTON. Oh, my God.

TANYA. To talk about my rights.

CARLTON. / Tanya…

SHONDA. No, you don't want a lawyer. You just want to shut up. You hear me? You just want to shut your mouth about all of this. Do you see that I'm just trying to do you a favor?

TANYA. Well, just don't *tell* anyone, then. Problem solved.

SHONDA. You're both gonna get me put in a camp.

CARLTON. So, then, you understand that there will be camps?

SHONDA. Shut up. The both of you. I ain't joking, now. *(Pause. She tries to return to her book. Then:) (to* **TANYA***)* How much is he paying you?

TANYA. Thought we weren't gonna talk about it.

SHONDA. 'Cause how's he gonna pay you if he's in jail?

TANYA. He's / got some friend in…

CARLTON. Tanya, please. *Please.* You're talking to the police right now.

SHONDA. I'm an administrative officer.

TANYA. *(to* **CARLTON***)* Anyway, I want fifty thousand dollars.

SHONDA. Fifty thousand dollars? For making a phone call? You / have got…

TANYA. Oh, there's a little more to it than / that, *believe* me.

CARLTON. Anyway, we weren't gonna talk about this, remember? Remember how dangerous it was to talk about this?

TANYA. She brought / it up.

CARLTON. But we just had that conversation.

(**SHONDA** *goes to the doorway to make sure they're safe.* **CARLTON** *mouths to* **TANYA** *"Yes! Fifty thousand! Yes!"*)

SHONDA. The Chief's in his office. *(to* CARLTON*)* Are they gonna arrest me?

CARLTON. If you don't help me stop them, then yes, they'll probably arrest you.

(**SHONDA** *considers it, decides he's bluffing.*)

SHONDA. They're not gonna arrest me.

CARLTON. How do you know?

SHONDA. For one thing, the Chief wouldn't allow it.

TANYA. And I want a pardon from the president.

CARLTON. I'm begging you…

TANYA. She don't know what we're talking about. I could be talking about anything.

CARLTON. Ms. Cox, could I have some water, please?

SHONDA. No. *(to* TANYA*)* A pardon for what?

TANYA. Really, it ain't none of your business, Shonda. Sorry / about that.

SHONDA. How you gonna get a presidential pardon?

TANYA. The new president, I mean. When everything's back to normal.

CARLTON. I'm sure you'll get whatever you want, Tanya. / Hypothetically speaking.

TANYA. I want a pardon, like Patty Hearst.

SHONDA. *(to* CARLTON*)* You gonna give her a presidential pardon?

CARLTON. I'm sure she won't need one, since, as far as I know, she's not intending to do anything illegal.

SHONDA. ...Like Patty Hearst?

CARLTON. As I've said, according to the accepted laws / of the land...

TANYA. *(to* **SHONDA***)* You got something against Patty Hearst?

SHONDA. I haven't got a thing against that rich white girl. But if I robbed some banks, you think I'd get a presidential pardon?

TANYA. She was brainwashed.

SHONDA. I grew up in East St. Louis. You think I wasn't brainwashed? I was brainwashed by everybody I ever saw. But I didn't rob anybody. If I'da got kidnapped off some street corner in East St. Louis and then turned up robbing banks, you think I woulda got a pardon from the president?

TANYA. She was locked in a closet for like a month.

SHONDA. I was locked in a closet, too. It's called East St. Louis, Illinois. For like fifteen years.

TANYA. Oh, boy. You / people are such babies about everything.

SHONDA. *(to* **CARLTON***)* So if you're gonna give her a pardon, you better make sure *everybody* gets a pardon, that's all I'm saying.

CARLTON. Okay, I'll definitely pass that along / to the next president, when I see him.

TANYA. And do I look rich to you anyway? I'm a poor white girl, missy, that's an oppressed fucking minority. My life is way more fucked up than yours, / but I try to say one thing, it's like "shut up, bitch, you ain't black."

SHONDA. I'm making something with my life because I *chose* to do so. I'm not responsible for your problems. But white people cannot always say the same about / black people and that's not a double standard, that's just the way it is.

TANYA. Oh, here we go. Blame / *whitey*, Shonda. Blame *whitey*.

CARLTON. Kill me now, please. Can someone please just kill me now?

(A dismayed **SWENSON** *has appeared in the doorway.)*

SWENSON. What are you doing, Shonda?

SHONDA. *(abashed)* Nothing.

SWENSON. Can you help me out here for a minute?

SHONDA. Yes.

(She exits.)

SWENSON. *(to* **TANYA***)* We're tryin' to get you out of here as fast as we can. In the meantime, maybe you should go back to sleep or something.

(He goes.)

CARLTON. Are you out of your mind? Why don't you / just tell her the whole plan?

TANYA. Shut up. I didn't tell her nothin'. But I don't know when we're gonna get these opportunities, and I want fifty thousand dollars and I want my pardon, and that's all.

CARLTON. Do you understand what you have to do?

TANYA. Yeah, man, I got to do some revolutionary shit. But revolutionaries gotta get paid, dude, that's what it's all about. So don't be Jewish about the money, is all I'm saying.

Now you're gonna say you're Jewish.

CARLTON. Yes.

TANYA. It's a figure of speech.

CARLTON. I understand. I've got bigger concerns right now.

TANYA. You're not the first Jew I ever saw.

CARLTON. I didn't think I was.

TANYA. I even had a thing with a Jew for awhile.

CARLTON. Do you remember what you're going to do?

TANYA. Yes, Carlton, I do. But I was gonna say, I bet I know what you're thinking.

CARLTON. Huh?

TANYA. "If I play my cards right."

CARLTON. What?

TANYA. I said I had a thing with a Jew; I bet you're thinking "If I play my cards right," you know?

CARLTON. *(bewildered)* I'm not, uh...

TANYA. "...Then I can, too."

I mean, "*She* will." That's *you* talking, is the idea. *(becoming increasingly self-conscious)* "She will *again*," you're saying. "Have a thing with a Jew."

"With *me*."

(finally)

You're not a fag, are you?

CARLTON. Yeah.

TANYA. *Fuck*, man. You're fucking kidding me. I'm in fucking cahoots with a fucking gay Jew, now. You're not gonna tell me you're Islamic now, are you?

CARLTON. No, I'm not an Islamic Jew.

TANYA. Thank God, man. Just don't fucking talk to me anymore. You're on my last fucking nerve.

(She's covering her embarrassment with, of course, hostility.)

(Muffled voices off.)

CARLTON. But you're going to help me?

(No response.)

Tanya, will you do what I'm asking?

TANYA. Just shut the fuck up.

Fucking kike-fag.

(A melancholy pause.)

SWENSON. *(off)* File this, please.

SHONDA. *(off)* Okay, um...hold on. Let me...

SWENSON. *(off)* Take it up to the desk. Thank you.

*(**SWENSON** enters, goes to **TANYA***'s cell, unlocks it.)*

You all sobered up now?

TANYA. I was never drunk.

SWENSON. Well, you just gotta fill out some paperwork and you can go.

TANYA. You never understood my situation.

SWENSON. Lot of books have been written on *that* subject.

TANYA. Whatever that means.

CARLTON. Tanya?

*(She exits, not looking at **CARLTON**. **SWENSON** starts to follow.)*

SWENSON. *(to **CARLTON**)* You holding up all right?

CARLTON. I could have just gone on with my life, you know.

SWENSON. Maybe you should have.

*(**SWENSON** exits.)*

*(**CARLTON** slumps, defeated.)*

*(After a moment, **SHONDA** enters.)*

SHONDA. Do you want something? Do you want some water or something?

Have you stopped speaking now?

Well, it's about time. I'm just playing.

Anyway, you'll be out of here soon. They called and said they're on the ground.

So…

I'm sure everything's gonna be all right. Right?

Everything's gonna be all right?

Right?

(blackout)

END OF ACT ONE.

ACT TWO

(A few hours later.)

(The main room of the police station. The door to the street is stage left. Upstage right is a hallway that leads to the restrooms and, beyond that, to the back door of the building. Downstage right is the door to a storage room. The door to the holding cells is up center. Right now it's ajar.)

(SHONDA *sits at a desk. Her book is open in front of her, but really she's listening to the voices coming from the holding room. As in Act One, the voices range from indistinct to unintelligible.)*

PITTMAN. *(off)* How could you put it on the internet, Carlton?

CARLTON. *(off)* It needed to be done.

PITTMAN. *(off)* No, I mean how could you succeed in doing that? We've checked all your activity.

CARLTON. *(off)* I'm just smarter than you.

LEE. *(off)* He's lying. He couldn't have done it.

PITTMAN. *(off)* Lying's a bad idea, Berg. You know why?

CARLTON. *(off)* Why?

PITTMAN. *(off) (unintelligible)*

LEE. *(off)* Is it on a flash-drive?

CARLTON. *(off) (unintelligible)*

PITTMAN. *(off)* I'm getting scared for you, Berg.

LEE. *(off) (unintelligible)*

PITTMAN. *(off)* Oh, we absolutely will, Bob. If that's what Carlton wants. Is that what you want, Carlton?

LEE. *(off)* He's not saying.

PITTMAN. *(off)* It's got to be in the car.

LEE. *(off)* Is it, Berg?

PITTMAN. *(off)* This is all about to go south on you, Berg. Okay, do him a big favor, will you, Bob? Go look in the car again.

LEE. *(off)* Are you serious?

PITTMAN. *(off)* Yeah. If you find it, he gets to go back home in one piece.

LEE. *(off)* Maybe.

PITTMAN *(off)* You hear that, Carlton? Everybody's mad at you now.

*(**LEE** enters. **SHONDA** pretends to be reading.)*

Close that door, will you?

*(**LEE** closes the door.)*

LEE. Excuse me, Shonda? When do you go home?

SHONDA. The Chief asked me to wait till he gets back.

LEE. When will that be?

SHONDA. I don't know.

LEE. Can I prop that back door open?

SHONDA. It'll make an alarm if you do.

LEE. If I knock, will you let me back in?

SHONDA. Uh huh. Is he all right in there?

LEE. Compared to what?

*(**LEE** exits down the hallway. **SHONDA** tiptoes toward the holding-room door. Just as she leans toward it, the door to the outside opens, startling her.)*

*(**TANYA** enters. She's trying to cover her nerves, and seems more subdued than we're used to seeing her.)*

TANYA. Excuse me, Ms. Cox.

SHONDA. What the hell are you doing here?

TANYA. Oh, that's nice. This is still a public building, isn't it? Don't my tax monies pay for this?

SHONDA. What do you want?

TANYA. I want my bag, girl. You got my bag in there somewhere.

SHONDA. You're *holding* a bag.

TANYA. Well, not this bag, obviously. Duh. Like, a purse. I had a purse with me when I came in.

SHONDA. It didn't say anything about that in your paperwork.

TANYA. Well, that's 'cause mistakes happen. So, if you got my purse somewhere, I just need to get that from you.

SHONDA. If I had anything like that, it would be in that back room.

TANYA. Well, all right, then.

SHONDA. I was just in there. There's no purse in there.

TANYA. How do you know?

SHONDA. 'Cause it's mostly old files and a bunch of junk, and one shelf where we throw people's stuff for safekeeping, and there's nothing on that shelf right now.

TANYA. Maybe it fell on the floor.

SHONDA. I don't think so.

TANYA. If you're too lazy to go look, just give me the key.

SHONDA. I told you I was just in there.

TANYA. Can't you go look?

> *(Under* **TANYA***'s careful gaze,* **SHONDA** *goes to one of the desks, opens the middle drawer, and removes a key. She unlocks the storage room, goes inside for two seconds, then re-emerges.)*

SHONDA. I searched high and low. No purse.

TANYA. Hm.

> *(***SHONDA** *closes the storage room door and returns the key to the desk.)*

Oh, well. I guess I left it somewhere else.

SHONDA. I guess you did.

TANYA. Okay. Thanks anyway.

*(She starts to go. **SHONDA** is suspicious.)*

SHONDA. Hold on a second. What are you up to?

TANYA. What am I *up* to? What? Huh? That makes *no* sense. You're a weird person, you know? Good bye.

(She exits.)

*(**SHONDA** thinks over the preceding events. Then she goes to the desk and removes the key. She opens a filing cabinet and hides the key in the back of the drawer. The instant she closes the drawer, the main door opens, startling her–again.)*

*(**TANYA** enters.)*

Hello, again. Sorry. I just had a quick question I wanted to follow up on, about something you said?

SHONDA. What is it?

TANYA. I really need to find my purse, you know? And you said you looked in there and everything, you know, and that's great. But you also said that there wasn't anything in there. Remember? But I remember that guy in there, Carlton or whatever, saying stuff about having a...like...*phone?* And some keys, or something, and like a laptop and some other shit, or whatever...? So, if there wasn't nothing in there, maybe my purse is wherever *that* guy's stuff is.

SHONDA. Is that what you're trying to do?

TANYA. I'm trying to get my purse, yeah. Why?

SHONDA. Tanya, those federal agents took all that stuff.

TANYA. What federal agents?

SHONDA. They're here right now. One of 'em's back there with that Carlton, and the other one's out in the impound. You need to just get the hell out of here and forget about this nonsense. These guys are up to some serious business, Tanya.

TANYA. Do you think they might put all that stuff back in that room later? I'm just asking because of my purse.

SHONDA. Tanya, this country is in, like, the biggest crisis of all time, ever, and the news people can't even go into Washington to show it. They got checkpoints on the highways, and curfews in the cities, and who *knows* what else. So, Tanya, whatever you think you're doing, I really don't think there's gonna be anybody around to pay you for it. Now, you had a long day. Why don't you just go home?

TANYA. Okay. All interesting stuff, but I'm gonna ask you to *focus*, Shonda. I was asking you if they were gonna put that stuff back in the room.

SHONDA. What do you think you're gonna do?

TANYA. I'm trying to get my *purse*, girl. Damn.

SHONDA. Do you want me to go in there and ask Agent Pittman if he has your purse?

TANYA. No, don't do *that*.

SHONDA. Why not?

TANYA. I'll just come back later and see if it's in that room.

SHONDA. Why don't I just ask him?

TANYA. Okay, Shonda, I fucking get it. You're a genius fucking detective, all right? I'll share the moolah with you if you'll just get me that fuckin' laptop, all right?

SHONDA. Did I tell you these men are not playing? If that thing disappears from this place, they're gonna know I had something to do with it.

(**TANYA** *pulls a gun from her bag.* **SHONDA** *is frightened.*)

TANYA. Do you know how to use a gun?

SHONDA. No.

TANYA. I do. Do you think I could kill them?

SHONDA. Do *you?*

TANYA. I don't know.

SHONDA. Well, you can't. Were you thinking about using that?

TANYA. Fuck yeah.

SHONDA. *(warily)* You gonna use that on me?

TANYA. *(cryptically)* It's the revolution.

SHONDA. Maybe it just *looks* like the revolution. Maybe if we just keep our heads about us, it will eventually turn out *not* to have been the revolution. Maybe smarter people than us are working this stuff out right now.

TANYA. They had their fuckin' chance, dude. They can't work out shit. I say we settle this shit right here in Lodus, Missouri. Now, I ain't ever killed anyone, but there's a first time for any shit, and goddammit, Shonda, I just fucking *feel* like it. You understand me?

SHONDA. Well…yeah.

TANYA. I won't stand around and do nothing anymore. Goddammit, I ain't invisible. You hear me?

(The upstage door opens. **TANYA** *ducks behind the front desk as* **PITTMAN** *appears.)*

PITTMAN. Where's the Chief?

SHONDA. He… He's still on checkpoint duty.

PITTMAN. Why don't you go home?

SHONDA. I told him I'd wait till he got back.

PITTMAN. He'll understand if you go home. I'll take responsibility.

SHONDA. I told him I'd stay.

PITTMAN. You know, this is kind of *our* police station now. That would be one way to look at it.

SHONDA. I guess I'll go then.

PITTMAN. Great. But could you call the Chief, first, and tell him to drop what he's doing? It's getting late, and I'd like to talk to him one more time before we go. Thanks.

(He returns to the holding room, and closes the door.)

*(*TANYA *emerges.)*

TANYA. Thanks for not busting me.

SHONDA. You better get out of here.

TANYA. Unh uh. *You* better get out of here. I'll give you five
   minutes to get clear.

SHONDA. And then what?

TANYA. I'm gonna go in there and get that laptop, and get
   Carlton out of there, too.

SHONDA. They will kill you.

TANYA. There's only one guy in there, right? I'm gonna kill
   that government fucker, and if the other one comes
   in, he won't know what hit him.

SHONDA. That sounds good.

TANYA. Really?

SHONDA. Yeah. You better hurry, though. I'm gonna get
   my stuff.

TANYA. Now you're talkin', girl.

SHONDA. Yeah, don't waste any time, though.

TANYA. I won't.

SHONDA. Yeah, let me get my... Oh, hold on, Tanya. Let
   me see the gun for a second.

TANYA. The gun?

   (But SHONDA has already taken it from her hand.)

SHONDA. Now get the fuck out of here.

TANYA. Bitch!

SHONDA. Go on. Before I arrest you and let them put you
   in some secret dungeon somewhere, you dumbass
   hoosier!

TANYA. You don't even know how to use that. I will kick
   your ass and take it right back from you.

SHONDA. You don't want to do that, or you would have
   done it already.

TANYA. Don't be so sure.

SHONDA. No, I *am* sure. You don't even *want* this gun. Do
   you *want* this gun?

TANYA. Yes.

SHONDA. That was a "yes" that sounded like a "no." Now
   get out of here before I yell for someone.

TANYA. Fuck you. I would take that fuckin' gun from you, except you would probably just yell for somebody, or something.

SHONDA. So go on, then.

TANYA. Don't you want to be in the revolution, Shonda?

SHONDA. For the millionth time, no, I do not.

TANYA. Well, I do. I *do* want to be in it. I ain't leavin'.

(We hear knocking at the back door.)

SHONDA. That's the other one, Tanya. Go on, now.

TANYA. I don't give a shit. I'm gonna stay here and fight for my country.

SHONDA. Damn it, girl.

TANYA. I told you.

(More knocking.)

SHONDA. What do you want me to do?

TANYA. Put that laptop in the storage room where it's supposed to be fucking be, so I can fucking steal it.

SHONDA. How?

TANYA. I saw where you put the key.

SHONDA. I know, but how are / you gonna get the chance t—

*(***TANYA*** *runs for the back hallway as the knocking starts up again, very loudly.)*

TANYA. I'm gonna hide in the ladies' room!

(She exits down the hallway, just as **PITTMAN** *enters from the holding room, holding his cell phone.* **SHONDA** *barely has time to drop the gun in a wastebasket.)*

PITTMAN. Why is Bob texting me?

SHONDA. Sorry.

(She exits down the hallway, and we hear her push open the door.)

LEE. *(off)* I've been knocking.

*(***SHONDA*** *enters, followed by* **LEE**.*)*

SHONDA. I know. Sorry. The other agent told me to go home, so I was getting ready...

PITTMAN. That was like five minutes ago.

SHONDA. I know, but the other agent was outside, and he said that...I should...

LEE. *(to* PITTMAN*)* I / searched that whole...

PITTMAN. *(to* SHONDA*)* What'd the Chief say? Is he on his way?

SHONDA. Mmhm.

PITTMAN. "Mmhm," what.

SHONDA. He's on his way.

PITTMAN. Are you sure you called him?

SHONDA. What do you mean?

PITTMAN. Because you act like you didn't call him.

SHONDA. No, I called him, he... It didn't pick up.

PITTMAN. Then why did you say he was on his way?

SHONDA. If it, you know, if it doesn't pick up, that usually means he's on his way. Because he's driving.

PITTMAN. *What* was your name?

SHONDA. Shonda.

PITTMAN. Let me ask you something, Shondra: Do I look like I'm fucking around?

SHONDA. Shonda.

PITTMAN. Sorry. Shonda: Do I look like I'm fucking around?

SHONDA. No.

PITTMAN. That's because I'm not fucking around, Shonda. I don't know what kind of work ethic you're used to, b– Do you know what a work ethic is?

SHONDA. Yes.

PITTMAN. Well, I don't know what kind you're used to, but as long as I'm here you're gonna do what I tell you and you're gonna do it with diligence, you understand?

SHONDA. I work for the city of Lodus.

PITTMAN. Right now *I'm* the city of Lodus. As long as I'm here, I'm the whole fucking city, you understand? Both streets and all four street corners. You understand? If that seems odd to you, I can ask the Chief to explain it to you.

SHONDA. Okay.

PITTMAN. "Okay," what.

SHONDA. You can ask the Chief to explain it to me.

(Not the answer he expected, but he recovers.)

PITTMAN. Why don't you call him and I will?

(SHONDA goes to the desk to make the call.)

(to LEE) So you didn't find anything in the car.

LEE. No. But why do you always say "I"?

PITTMAN. In what sense?

LEE. "*I'm* the city of Lodus." "As long as *I'm* here." Can't you ever say "we"?

PITTMAN. I don't know if you want to be part of my dark speech or *not*, Bob.

LEE. Well, if it's something like declaring our authority or something, then of course I do. You make it look like I'm just your "henchman" or something.

PITTMAN. Can / I just say "okay" and move on?

SHONDA. *(on phone)* Chief? It's Shonda.

LEE. If you mean it.

PITTMAN. I do.

SHONDA. *(on phone)* They / want to know when you'll be back.

PITTMAN. Did you check the whole exterior of the car, underneath and everything?

LEE. Yes.

(PITTMAN whispers in LEE's ear.)

SHONDA. *(on phone)* Okay. I'm gonna tell 'em that. Bye.

(hangs up)

LEE. *(to* **PITTMAN***)* What do you mean?

PITTMAN. *(to* **SHONDA***)* You can go ahead, now. I'll see you tomorrow, if we're still here.

LEE. Let's hope not.

SHONDA. I told the Chief I'd stay.

PITTMAN. What did I just tell you about that?

SHONDA. You told me to ask the Chief to explain it to me.

PITTMAN. You really want to mess with me, don't you?

SHONDA. No. I don't want to mess with you.

PITTMAN. Wait for the Chief outside, then.

SHONDA. Maybe I should see if Mr. Berg needs something.

PITTMAN. Not necessary.

SHONDA. He shouldn't be alone for too long.

PITTMAN. He's fine. He's resting. Wait outside.

SHONDA. I...I...

PITTMAN. You *what.*

(*She makes a decision.*)

SHONDA. I just need to go to the ladies' room first.

(**LEE** *and* **PITTMAN** *watch all of the following with increasing impatience:*)

(**SHONDA** *starts for the hallway, stops.*)

Oh. I just need to...

(*She picks up a pile of papers from the desk, appears to examine them judiciously.*)

Hmm.

(*She dumps them all in the wastebasket [to cover the gun.] She starts again for the hallway, stops again, returns to the desk to get more papers, "examines" them, then stuffs them into the filing cabinet, from which she nonchalantly takes the keys. Then, trying not to hurry, she goes down the hallway.*)

LEE. Alone at last. So, *what* now?

PITTMAN. I gave him the thiopental.

LEE. Great. Let's get in there before he starts talking.

PITTMAN. It doesn't work like that. It'll just inhibit his... cortical blah blah, so he feels depressed. We'll let him think about things while he stands on his tippy-toes in there, and then we'll step it up to double super *special* enhanced interrogation. And if that doesn't work, I'm told we might have some *real* talent coming up from Little Rock.

LEE. CIA?

PITTMAN. The less you know, the better.

LEE. What does that mean?

PITTMAN. That's what people say to protect people.

LEE. I don't want to be protected, Dale.

PITTMAN. Don't start on this again, Bob. This is an extremely delicate situation.

LEE. I'm already *in* this situation. I think it gives you a sense of power to have these meetings without me.

PITTMAN. I'll try to include you in the meetings, Bob, if I can. But this is very unprofessional. I don't want to hear it anymore. Understand?

LEE. Do you understand *me?*

PITTMAN. Yes.

LEE. Then, yes.

PITTMAN. Good. Now, listen: If Swenson's got his mind straight, he can help us clean up the paper trail. But if he starts on this judge business again, I've got... Spalding gave me the name of a judge, she sings our song, you know? And she's like ten minutes away, so she's perfect.

LEE. She'll sign off on this?

PITTMAN. That's what I'm saying, Bob. Spalding says she's true blue.

TANYA. *(off)* Fuck 'em!

(They both heard that, and turn to the door.)

(SHONDA anxiously peeks out of the restroom to find them staring at her.)

PITTMAN. Giving yourself a little pep talk?

(SHONDA enters, while making a bit of a show of clearing her throat.)

Did you get that out of your system?

(She ignores him, looks for a stall, finds another stack of papers.)

Could you wait outside?

(Defeated, she puts down the papers.)

SHONDA. *(re: CARLTON)* Maybe he needs something to eat, or something.

PITTMAN. What did I say about that?

SHONDA. Maybe he stopped resting.

PITTMAN. You're not gonna see him.

LEE. Enough is enough, Shonda.

(SWENSON enters from the street.)

PITTMAN. Ah hah. There's your boss. You can run along, now. Thanks.

SHONDA. You said he was gonna explain something to me first.

PITTMAN. Unbelievable.

SWENSON. What's goin' on?

SHONDA. This man says you're gonna tell me who's in charge here.

SWENSON. Is there a problem?

SHONDA. I just want to know who's in charge.

SWENSON. Well, this being a national security issue…*they* are. You know that.

PITTMAN. That's right.

SHONDA. Okay. I just wanted to know, and he said ask you.

SWENSON. Right. Well. It's a, it's a cooperative effort.

PITTMAN. And we appreciate that.

SWENSON. You're welcome.

SHONDA. *(to* **SWENSON***)* If you say so.

SWENSON. Well…why wouldn't I say so?

SHONDA. Because of the emergency making things so confusing.

LEE. That's why we have a written order from the attorney general of the United States.

SHONDA. Some people was saying he's not legitimate, so that's why I was wondering, is all.

LEE. Well, those people are wrong.

SWENSON. It's a matter of opinion, I guess.

LEE. A federal order is not a matter of opinion.

SWENSON. You don't need to worry, you're not gettin' any argument from us. She's just asking who's in charge, and I guess that's okay, right? That's what we're all asking.

LEE. Sure.

SHONDA. *(to* **SWENSON***)* Were you thinking about letting Carlton see a judge?

PITTMAN. Don't worry about "Carlton." "Carlton" is fine. Go home.

SWENSON. Hold on, now. Let's keep a civil tone. Now, I've been thinking that over, and I've made up my mind. If he wants a judge, I just don't see the harm in getting him one.

*(***PITTMAN*** fumes for a moment, then:)*

PITTMAN. Not a problem.

(He takes out his cell, locates a number.)

SWENSON. *(to* **SHONDA***)* You better go on now.

PITTMAN. *(to* **SWENSON***)* Good luck with that.

SHONDA. I have some more questions.

SWENSON. You better ask me your questions tomorrow. Go on, now.

PITTMAN. *(angry)* You know what? *(but he's interrupted by voicemail)* Hello, my name is Dale Pittman, I'm with the

Department of Homeland Security, this is a message for Judge Eleanor Wurlitz, I believe you already spoke to Sp– to a colleague of mine, ahmm, could you call me at this number or stop by the Lodus police station, it's very important. Thank you. *(hangs up) (to* **SWENSON***)* Okay?

SWENSON. Judge Wurlitz, huh?

PITTMAN. You know her?

SWENSON. Not real well. I've seen her around, you know?

PITTMAN. So, no problems, then?

SWENSON. I guess not.

PITTMAN. Great. Can we dispense with your employee now?

SWENSON. *(to* **SHONDA***)* What the hell, Shonda.

SHONDA. I have a concern.

SWENSON. What is it?

SHONDA. We're not supposed to give away the evidence.

SWENSON. What evidence?

SHONDA. All of his stuff. The suspect's stuff.

SWENSON. Why don't you let me worry about that?

SHONDA. It breaks the chain of custody.

SWENSON. They think he might have some state secrets.

SHONDA. But we're not supposed to just give it to them.

SWENSON. I thought we just covered this, Shonda. I talked to their superior on the phone. Like we've been saying, these are emergency circumstances.

SHONDA. All the more reason, it seems to me, not to just talk to somebody on the phone.

PITTMAN. *Shonda.* It's all going to come to the same thing.

SHONDA. I understand that. In the meantime, that's our evidence.

LEE. Fine. Who cares, Dale? We checked all that shit anyway.

PITTMAN. We checked it, yeah, but we haven't, you know, *checked* it. We need to get that laptop back to Washington and pull it apart. Let the *experts* look at it.

SWENSON. I think there's something in what Shonda says.

PITTMAN. That's our stuff, Chief. The deal's done. Chain of custody is broken anyway; the stuff's worthless to you.

SWENSON. Still and all.

PITTMAN. There's no crime here for you to investigate. It's strictly a national security issue.

SWENSON. She's right, though. We made the arrest.

PITTMAN. Alright, do you want to talk to Washington again?

SWENSON. I don't see how that's necessary.

PITTMAN. I didn't think so.

SWENSON. I mean, because it won't do you any good. I'm gonna keep the stuff till I get a writ for it.

PITTMAN. Let's get something straight, Chief. We've been trying to show due courtesy and all, but I think we let you forget who we are. Now, I can make a phone call and come back with a presidential order to arrest you–both of you–throw you both in your own fucking jail and take whatever I fucking-well please.

LEE. And when he says "I," he means "we," just to clarify.

SWENSON. I can make phone calls, too.

PITTMAN. Who are *you* gonna call, Chief?

SWENSON. I'm gonna call some dumb, crazy redneck friends of mine and tell 'em there's a couple of bureaucrats from Washington here to take their guns away.

Now, I'm a good American, and I want to work with you guys, but this conversation just seems to be going around in a circle. So here's what I'm gonna do: I'm gonna interpret these quandaries as I go, in light of what I think is probably best for the country, and I just don't see how anybody can blame me for that.

That ain't too nuanced for you boys, is it?

(pause)

LEE. *(to PITTMAN)* Can the judge give us that writ?

PITTMAN. *(to* **SWENSON***)* Can she?

SWENSON. Yeah.

PITTMAN. *(to* **LEE***)* Great. Go get the bag.

> *(***LEE** *exits to the holding room, returns with a gym bag. He drops it in front of* **SWENSON.***)*

> *(***PITTMAN** *takes a scrap of paper from his pocket, hands it to* **LEE.***)*

Now, go to that judge's house and see if she's home. If she is, get her here ASAP.

LEE. What if she doesn't want to come?

PITTMAN. You're Homeland Security, goddammit. If she doesn't piss her panties, you're not doing your job.

LEE. Just wanted to make sure.

> *(***LEE** *exits.)*

SWENSON. Shonda, go ahead and put this bag in evidence, will you please?

> *(***SHONDA** *picks up the bag and carries it to the storage room.)*

PITTMAN. It's been a long day for everybody, right?

SWENSON. Yeah.

PITTMAN. These are unusual circumstances.

> *(***SHONDA** *realizes, with horror, that she can't open the door. She gave the key to* **TANYA.***)*

SWENSON. You forget the key?

> *(He moves toward the desk.)*

SHONDA. I'll get it.

> *(She heads for the desk.)*

PITTMAN. But I know you were bluffing. You wouldn't have called your friends on us.

SWENSON. I would if I had to.

> *(At the desk,* **SHONDA** *pretends to collect the key.)*

PITTMAN. You'd have been starting a lot of trouble.

SWENSON. I would if I had to.

SHONDA. Oh! I feel sick!

SWENSON. What's the matter?

(**SHONDA** *runs off down the hallway.*)

PITTMAN. What was that about?

SWENSON. I don't know.

PITTMAN. Well, now I feel like I brought you back here for nothing.

SWENSON. Oh, I think we got a lot accomplished.

PITTMAN. Not what I had in mind, though.

SWENSON. Guess not, no.

PITTMAN. So if you want to get back out there...

(**SHONDA** *enters.*)

SWENSON. You all right?

SHONDA. Yeah, I guess it was all the nervous excitement. I just need to...

(She unlocks the storage room.)

SWENSON. I'll take care of that.

SHONDA. Just a sec.

SWENSON. Shonda...

SHONDA. *(snapping)* I'm not leavin' those things out here!

SWENSON. Holy cow.

(**SHONDA** *gets the bag and lugs it into the storage room. She emerges a moment later, locking the door behind her.*)

Okay?

SHONDA. Yeah. It's all in there.

SWENSON. Good night.

SHONDA. Did I leave my purse in the restroom?

(She heads for the women's room.)

SWENSON. No. It's right there. Shonda?

(But she's gone.)

(A second later, she re-emerges [without the key].)

SHONDA. No, you're right. There it is.

(She picks up her coat and purse.)

SWENSON. Just put the key back, before we both forget.

(She freezes.)

SHONDA. Um.

SWENSON. Shonda?

SHONDA. Hm?

SWENSON. Just put the key back, before we both forget.

SHONDA. I don't feel good!

(She drops everything and runs into the women's room.)

PITTMAN. This / is ridiculous.

SWENSON. What in the world…?

(From the women's room, we hear faint sounds that could be construed as a struggle.)

PITTMAN. Is she pregnant or something?

SWENSON. Not that I know of.

(SHONDA emerges, slightly disheveled, with the key.)

Are you throwing up?

SHONDA. No, I just feel woozy.

PITTMAN. Go home and get some rest, maybe. I *insist.*

SWENSON. I'm worried about you.

SHONDA. I told you, it's just the nerves.

(Confidently, and a bit ostentatiously, she returns the key to its place.)

SWENSON. Good night, then.

(SHONDA collects her things again.)

SHONDA. *(rather loudly)* I put all Mr. Berg's stuff in the back room, and I put the key back…

(She remembers the gun in the wastebasket, removes the liner bag, takes it with her.)

…So that's it for me, I guess.

SWENSON. Yeah. Good night.

SHONDA. Bye. *(sincerely)* Thank you, Chief.

SWENSON. Thank *you*.

(**SHONDA** *exits.*)

PITTMAN. So, I'm saying: He sees a judge, the judge sees his socks and underwear, we got it all worked out in record time…so if you want to get back on patrol, I think that's a great idea.

SWENSON. What's gonna happen to Berg?

PITTMAN. Come on, Chief. He's a piece of shit.

SWENSON. Maybe. But what's gonna happen to him?

PITTMAN. The fact that you're asking that shows you just why we've got to put him out of the way for a little while. He's poisonous. He's infecting everyone's minds with crazy conspiracy theories. This database he's got, it's meaningless. It's *theoretical*. You can read about it on the internet. Getting that thing back, it's not the tenth most…it's not the *fiftieth* most important thing we have to do right now, with all the shit that's going on out there. But there is still such a thing as treason, Chief, and goddammit, he's a traitor to his country.

SWENSON. He seems to think he's in the resistance or something.

PITTMAN. Exactly. Same thing, right? Except, who is he resisting? The heroes who have stepped up to restore law and order. Let me tell you something, Chief: I work with those guys every day, and they might seem pretty tough and ruthless to you and me, but I've seen how much they care. I've seen them cry for their country. I've seen the tears in their eyes. Once you've seen that, I tell you, you know where to stand.

Now, please: Get out on that checkpoint, let people take comfort in seeing you, guys like you…*out* there, you know? And let me handle things here, all right?

SWENSON. The judge might come by, the phones might ring…

PITTMAN. I'll stay out here till Agent Lee comes back, all right? Settled.

SWENSON. All right. I'll see you in a while, if you're still here. Call me if you have to leave.

PITTMAN. You got it.

SWENSON. *(nodding toward the holding room)* He might need to use the john or something.

PITTMAN. I'll take care of him.

SWENSON. *(shrugs)* He's your prisoner.

PITTMAN. That's right.

(SWENSON starts to go.)

And, hey: Call *me* if you're on your way back, will you?

(SWENSON stops, considers this. Exits.)

(PITTMAN goes straight for the holding room.)

PITTMAN. *(off)* How are you, Carlton? What's that? Not talking?

(TANYA peers out from the hallway. She inches into the room, tiptoeing toward the desk with the key.)

Come on, buddy.

(Sounds of the cell being unlocked.)

(TANYA freezes, then dashes back down the hallway just as PITTMAN shoves CARLTON into the room.)

(CARLTON has been drugged, and it's taken all the fight out of him. He's haggard and disoriented.)

(PITTMAN shoves him into a chair and handcuffs him to a bracket on the desk. He snaps his fingers in front of CARLTON's face and checks the dilation of his eyes.)

PITTMAN. Are you with me, pal? Has that stuff loosened your brain a little? Because I need your attention.

(He goes to the window and lowers the blinds.)

I need one-hundred-percent of your attention. *(He pulls out a stun gun.)* I call this guy Scalia. In memory of the greatest Supreme Court Justice ever. Because according to Scalia, God rest his soul wherever he may be, torture can't be cruel and unusual punishment, because it isn't *punishment*, see? As long as I'm asking questions, my goal is not to punish you; it's just to get information. Isn't that great? So, you see, it's a vicious lie that we threw out the Constitution. The Constitution is still working great for us.

Now, what's the capital of Djibouti?

(He moves in on **CARLTON***, ready to strike.)*

*(***TANYA*** peeks out from the hallway.* **CARLTON** *sees her and tries to communicate with her.)*

CARLTON. Yes! Yes!

PITTMAN. *(momentarily arrested)* I gotta tell you, that's not the response I expected.

(He moves in again.)

CARLTON. Ahhhh! Shit! You should be struck down! Goddammit, you should be struck down with something heavy!

PITTMAN. Like what, *ennui?* Just tell me where the flash-drive is, okay?

*(***TANYA***, getting the message, has picked up a coffee mug.)*

CARLTON. No! Not that! That will not do the job!

(But **TANYA** *approaches* **PITTMAN***, wielding the mug.)*

PITTMAN. Let's see, okay?

(He drives the stun gun into **CARLTON***'s groin.* **CARLTON** *screams.)*

(This takes the fight out of **TANYA***. She backs toward the hallway, still clutching the mug.)*

CARLTON. No! Please! Please help me, I'm begging you!

(But she's too scared. She retreats to the restroom.)

PITTMAN. I'm *trying* to help you. But you've got to help me, too. I didn't come out to the fucking Ozarks to kill you, Berg. If we wanted to do that, we could have paid that hillbilly sheriff a thousand dollars to take care of it *for* us. No, I came down here to bring you back to civilization. *If* you cooperate. If you *don't* cooperate, I will shoot you dead right here. And me and my partner will get back in our Crown Vic and go back to Washington. Leaving you right here on this floor, because we don't even have to dispose of your corpse. It's a new world, pal. One without consequences for us.

CARLTON. That's a fantasy. Even if your guys stay in power, they're gonna have to explain all this shit one day. That's why they picked you in the first place. Because you're crass and degenerate and easy to explain. You've got lollipop written all over your face.

*(**PITTMAN** stuns **CARLTON**. **CARLTON** screams.)*

Ow! Shit! You didn't ask a question!

*(**PITTMAN** takes out his cell phone.)*

PITTMAN. *(absently, looking for a number)* What's the capital of…Burkina Faso?

CARLTON. Ouagadougou.

PITTMAN. Really?

CARLTON. Yes.

PITTMAN. No shit?

CARLTON. Yeah.

PITTMAN. There's two more questions.

*(He stuns him. **CARLTON** screams.)*

(re: the phone) This fucking thing.

(He sits at a desk, his back to the hallway, and picks up the phone on the desk. He dials a number that he reads off his cell phone.)

We're out of time, Berg. We need to get that writ, or subpoena, or whatever it is, and get out of Dogpatch,

U.S.A. But I'm not...*(on phone)* Dale Pittman. I need to speak to Spalding. *(to* **CARLTON***)* I'm not putting you in the system. I won't have it. Fucking Andy Griffith and everybody else can kiss my ass, because I'm not allowing you in the system. You're not talking to anybody but us. And if...*(on phone)* Yep. Thanks. *(to* **CARLTON***)* And if you don't feel like talking to us, well...

(He lets the implication hang there.)

(Exhausted, **CARLTON** *puts his head down on the desk.)*

PITTMAN. *(cont.) (on phone)* I need to speak to Spalding. Because I need to know what I'm supposed to do with Berg.

Well, where's the CIA?

Why the fuck not, Dennis?

They're waiting for *what?*

Oh, what pussies they are. So, they're *out.*

What that means is that they're out, so fuck 'em. Let's move on. What do I do with Berg?

On what authority?

On... No, on what authority?

*(***TANYA,*** still armed with the coffee mug, enters from the hallway.)*

Exactly. So...okay. Here's what I need to know: Are we killing people?

(She creeps up behind **PITTMAN***.)*

*(***LEE*** enters through the main door. With no place to hide,* **TANYA** *freezes—in plain sight of* **LEE***, but unseen by* **PITTMAN***.* **TANYA** *assumes a casual pose.* **LEE***, momentarily surprised, now sees a colleague waiting, coffee mug in hand, for* **PITTMAN** *to finish his call.* **LEE** *approaches the desk.)*

(to **LEE***)* Was she home?

LEE. No. There was no ans–

PITTMAN. *(on phone)* But I don't want you to assume anything. See? I want to know if we are, as an official adjunct of our...if we are officially killing people. See?

*(**LEE** nods to **TANYA**, who nods back.)*

Then I need that in writing.

No sir. I am not standing up for some Abu Ghraib bullshit.

LEE. *(to **TANYA**)* I'm / Robert Lee.

PITTMAN. *(on phone)* I need a cl– *(to **LEE**)* Yeah yeah.

*(**PITTMAN** waves for silence. **TANYA** nods again to **LEE**, jabs a thumb toward **PITTMAN**, shrugs: "Whatta ya gonna do?")*

(on phone) ...A clear, written declaration, describing the, no, *setting* the parameters of our...

*(**LEE** is shooting curious glances at **TANYA**, who is trying to discourage conversation.)*

No, I'm telling you. Here's what I want: I want one, specific, written order on what to do with Berg. Because if this thing goes *south*...

Yeah, because history has no turnings, right? But if this whole plan goes *south*, I am not taking the, sorry... *(acknowledging **LEE**)* Robert Lee and I are not taking the rap. We're going to have a signed order, author–in fact, *telling* us–how to dispose of Berg.

*(**CARLTON** raises his head; takes in the scene, befuddled.)*

Signed by *Spalding*, goddammit. What's the matter with you? Or higher, actually. The *president* would be great.

Well, if he thinks he's / doing some–

CARLTON. What in the *fuck*?

(A beat)

PITTMAN. *(on phone)* If he thinks he's doing something wrong, then we better all drop what we're doing and start calling our lawyers, right?

*(He exchanges looks with **LEE**, who passes the exchange to **TANYA**, who nods appreciatively.)*

PITTMAN. *(cont.)* So are we killing people, or not?

I don't know either, so send me the order.

Fax it.

Well, that's up to you guys. If you want us to bring him back, we're not gonna leave till morning, anyway. If you want us to continue interrogating him, we can go all night. If you want us to kill him, well, that's *your* timeline.

Hm. Email it, too, that's fine, but fax it, so it comes through this...station, here. So... Because I want it in the cache. I want it traceable.

Because I know how you guys are, Dennis, come *on.* No offense.

(LEE takes a step away from the desk, hoping to draw TANYA away for a conversation. He indicates CARLTON.)

LEE. *(very quietly, to TANYA)* Have you...?

(Both PITTMAN and TANYA cut him off with a "Just a second" gesture.)

PITTMAN. You bet your ass I'm covering my ass. But don't characterize it as... Yes. Yes. Fine. "Are we killing people?" That's all. We'll be waiting for that fax.

All right. Bye.

(Hangs up. To LEE) What's up?

LEE. I don't know. What *is* up?

PITTMAN. Well. You heard.

LEE. *(re: TANYA)* So we're ratcheting things up around here.

PITTMAN. I wouldn't say that. It's all part of the plan. We're just making sure the paperwork is in place.

LEE. Right. So bring me up to date.

PITTMAN. I just did. You heard everything. Why don't you go over to that Super 8 and get us a couple of rooms?

LEE. Are you dismissing me?

PITTMAN. What?

LEE. I'm not supposed to be part of this?

PITTMAN. Part of what?

LEE. Is that how we're playing it, Dale? Thanks.

PITTMAN. What is up your ass now, Bob? Or better yet, don't tell me. This is not the time.

(**TANYA** *glares menacingly at* **LEE**.)

LEE. *(sullenly)* Okay. I get it. I'm not needed. Sorry.

PITTMAN. When the judge gets here, I'll call you.

LEE. Fine.

(*To* **TANYA**'*s horror,* **PITTMAN** *stands!*)

But until then, go get the rooms, huh?

(**PITTMAN**, *exiting to the holding cells, is focused on* **LEE**. **TANYA** *drifts to the filing cabinets, hoping to stay out of sight.*)

PITTMAN. Or better yet, just stay out here until that cop gets back and then, yes, go get the goddamn rooms at the Super 8. Whatever your problem is, Bob, let's just save it for later, okay? Let's focus.

(**PITTMAN** *exits to the holding cells.*)

LEE. *(to* **TANYA***)* I guess I just don't like being / left out.

PITTMAN. *(off)* What?!

LEE. Nothing!

(**PITTMAN** *closes the door to the cells.* **TANYA** *nods pleasantly, sets down the mug, starts moving nonchalantly toward the main doors.*)

Are we gonna take care of him here, or...?

TANYA. Yeah.

LEE. Yeah?

TANYA. It's better we don't talk about it. Listen, / I gotta...

LEE. Look, even if Dale's being kind of a dick right now, can you keep me in the loop? As much as possible, I mean?

TANYA. Shit, yeah. Don't worry about it.

LEE. Thanks.

TANYA. Yeah. I gotta get some stuff from my car.

LEE. Okay. I'll keep an eye on him.

(a beat)

TANYA. Listen. Can you get me that laptop?

LEE. Berg's laptop?

TANYA. Yeah.

LEE. We already totally checked it.

TANYA. Yeah. Can I just have it?

LEE. Sure. *(on second thought)* I mean, you are the CIA person, right?

TANYA. *(shrugging: "Wish I could tell you.")* Dude.

LEE. Right. Um…*(thinks for a moment)* I need to ask Dale where they put it.

(He heads for the holding room.)

TANYA. In that back room. They said. *Carlton* said. Right, Carlton? The key's right here.

(She opens the desk drawer, takes the key, whips it to **LEE.***)*

So. Okay?

LEE. Sure.

*(***LEE*** exits to the storage room.)*

CARLTON. Eldard Mandrishevil.

TANYA. Shut up.

CARLTON. Don't come back for me.

TANYA. I won't.

*(***PITTMAN*** enters with his overnight bag.)*

PITTMAN. Can I help you?

TANYA. You must be Dale.

PITTMAN. Yeah. Dale Pittman. Judge Wurlitz?

TANYA. Judge Wurlitz.

PITTMAN. / You're…?

TANYA. Yeah. I'm Judge Wurlitz, I'm saying.

PITTMAN. Nice to meet / you.

TANYA. Yeah. What's up. What's…the occasion…of…

PITTMAN. Well, Bob explained our situation, I guess.

TANYA. Yeah, you're…Homeland…persons, and…

(A beat. She's got nothing else.)

PITTMAN. Yeah, we have a delicate national security situation here, and…

*(***LEE*** enters with the laptop.)*

…the Chief is being kind of a stickler, which is fine, we want to observe the, the rule of law here and all, and we were / hoping…

*(***LEE*** hands her the laptop.)*

TANYA. Thanks.

PITTMAN. What's going on?

LEE. She wanted Berg's laptop.

PITTMAN. Oh, okay. May I ask…?

TANYA. I gotta get some items out of my c– I'm totally on your guys' side. It's totally in…procedure, so…I'll be right back, you gentlemen.

PITTMAN. Sure, sure. But this writ we need…

TANYA. Uh huh.

*(***SWENSON*** enters from outside.)*

SWENSON. *(to ***TANYA***)* Now, what the hell are *you* doing here?

CARLTON. / Oh.

TANYA. Excuse me?

PITTMAN. Is there a problem, Chief?

TANYA. I'm / just leaving.

SWENSON. What does she want from you?

CARLTON. Oh.

PITTMAN. She's here to help us out and you need to not interfere with her, Chief.

SWENSON. How the hell is *she* gonna help you out?

LEE. / Chief…

TANYA. / Well…

PITTMAN. You wanted a judge and now you got a judge. / We're moving…

LEE. This is a federal matter now, and… *(to* **PITTMAN***)* What?

CARLTON. I mean…

TANYA. *(shutting everyone up)* Yeah! I'm the judge, motherfucker! That's why! 'Cause I'm the motherfucking JUDGE! So shut the fuck up, motherfucker! *(She's sidling towards the door.)* Now, I'm getting something from my autom– you fucking…

(And she's gone.)

(pause)

PITTMAN. That was eccentric.

SWENSON. What was she doing here?

CARLTON. I'm ready to talk!

PITTMAN. Oh, you are?

CARLTON. I'll tell you everything!

PITTMAN. We'll talk in private.

SWENSON. Hold / on a second.

CARLTON. *(to* **PITTMAN***)* Let's go in the back.

SWENSON. What was she doing here?

PITTMAN. You asked for a judge…

CARLTON. I'm telling you where the *thing* is.

LEE. Where?

CARLTON. Let's go in the back.

PITTMAN. In a minute. *(to* **SWENSON***)* You asked for a judge…

CARLTON. It's in the car.

LEE. Where in the car?

CARLTON. Under the… In the fuse box.

LEE. I *checked* the fuse boxes.

CARLTON. Under the…

LEE. *Both* of them.

SWENSON. What the hell are you guys up to?

PITTMAN. What are you up to? You tell us to get a judge, we get a judge, and then you come in talking shit. And I thought you were gonna call first.

SWENSON. Yeah, I guess that's just the part I didn't like.

CARLTON. Not the *fuse* box. The *other...*

PITTMAN. *(to CARLTON)* Just shut up a second. *(to LEE)* And what the holy shit is wrong with that woman?

CARLTON. The.../ The other thing that's...

LEE. That's what I'm w– Wait. You're saying she's a *judge?*

PITTMAN. Sh– She... What? *You're* saying she's a judge.

LEE. *(trying to play along)* Oh, oh. Yeah. When I said "You're saying she's a judge," I meant, "*You're* saying she's a judge? *I'm* saying she's a judge."

PITTMAN. *(baffled)* / What?!

CARLTON. Not the fuse box.

LEE. I remember now.

CARLTON. / The other...

PITTMAN. What the fuck are you talking about?

LEE. Aren't we...?

(A confused beat.)

CARLTON. Chief?

PITTMAN. I never introduced you to her.

LEE. Okay: I'm trying to play along, Dale, so: / Nice.

CARLTON. Chief, you gotta help me.

PITTMAN. Play along with what?

LEE. Jesus, you're horrible at this.

SWENSON. *(re: CARLTON)* What did you do to this man?

PITTMAN. I just gave him something to relax him.

SWENSON. He doesn't look relaxed to me.

CARLTON. No no, I'm *not.* I'm not / relaxed.

LEE. You're a cop. You know what we have to do.

SWENSON. What *who* has to do? Cops?

LEE. *Yeah,* / Chief.

CARLTON. I'm *not* / relaxed.

SWENSON. Is that what you think you are, a cop?

LEE. / Um…

PITTMAN. Hold on. Goddammit. Who just left here with that laptop?

CARLTON. *(to* **SWENSON***)* I don't deserve this. I don't / deserve this.

SWENSON. You're gonna be / okay now.

PITTMAN. Was that the judge, or not?

SWENSON. No, shit-for-brains, she was in lockup a few hours ago.

CARLTON. / Listen…

PITTMAN. What the fuck, Bob?

LEE. You told me she was CIA!

PITTMAN. / What?!

CARLTON. Listen…

LEE. I mean…

   (A confused beat.)

PITTMAN. Go get her! Get her!

   *(***LEE*** *exits.)*

CARLTON. Stop him, Chief.

SWENSON. *(to* **CARLTON***)* Just / calm down.

PITTMAN. She was in lockup? What?!

SWENSON. She was in for an outstanding warrant or something.

PITTMAN. And she came back here just to steal a laptop? *What?*

CARLTON. *(to* **PITTMAN***, reasonably)* No no / no. You've got it all…

SWENSON. You got me, buddy. I don't know what the hell has been going on here.

CARLTON. You've got it all wrong.

(**LEE** *enters.*)

LEE. She's gone.

PITTMAN. Of course she's gone. That's why you have to *chase* her.

LEE. She could be anywhere. I don't know this area.

CARLTON. Bob, / I remembered where the thing is now.

PITTMAN. Wake up, Chief! Wake up! We've got to get an APB out on her. County, State, / National Guard, everybody! The army, too. Let's go!

CARLTON. I want to talk in private!

LEE. What are we talking about, Dale?

CARLTON. / Bob.

PITTMAN. I don't know, Bob. I don't know if she's working for him, *(i.e.,* **CARLTON***)* I don't know if she's a wild... kleptomaniac... She told you she was a fucking judge. What?! / So...

LEE. No. You told *me* she was CIA.

CARLTON. / Bob.

PITTMAN. I most certainly did not. Carlton, clear this up for me. *(shaking him)* Carlton! can you see that we are *confused?!*

SWENSON. Don't handle him like that.

PITTMAN. Chief, what did I tell you? Now get on the phone or...however this is done, fucking *do* it! You understand?

SWENSON. I'm not worried about *her.* It's *you* I want to talk to.

PITTMAN. Was she working for you, Carlton? Talk to me!

(*He hits him.*)

SWENSON. All right, that's enough!

LEE. Chief, you got your *own* job to do.

SWENSON. What has she got? That Enemies' List?

PITTMAN. What / she's got...

LEE. They don't need to know what she's got. They / just need to hold her.

SWENSON. *I* want to know! Now, she's got the names of a bunch of American citizens that you want to round up. Is that right?

PITTMAN. That's classified.

(He exchanges a look with LEE.*)*

CARLTON. American citizens, going about / their lives…

SWENSON. American citizens, who as far as we know, haven't done a goddamn thing yet. Is that right?

PITTMAN. Are you *judging* me?

SWENSON. Is that right, Berg?

*(*LEE *moves to a position behind* SWENSON.*)*

PITTMAN. How dare / you.

CARLTON. Yes.

PITTMAN. Shut up, Berg. *(He goes to his bag.)* Be ready, Bob.

(He pulls a collapsible steel baton from his bag and extends it.)

CARLTON. People who just want to / oh *fuck* you've got to do something!

PITTMAN. Bob.

SWENSON. *(hand on sidearm)* That's not happening! Put it down!

*(*PITTMAN *approaches* CARLTON.*)*

Put / it down!

CARLTON. Behind you!

*(*LEE *draws his gun on* SWENSON.*)*

LEE. Hands up! / On your head! On your head!

*(*LEE *unholsters* SWENSON*'s sidearm.)*

CARLTON. Holy God, why didn't I go north?

SWENSON. You're out of your goddamn minds.

CARLTON. / Stupidest bunch of…

PITTMAN. *(to* CARLTON*)* Shut up, Berg.

CARLTON. …redneck…

PITTMAN. *(to* **SWENSON***)* Take off your belt.

SWENSON. You must be crazy.

PITTMAN. I'm embarrassed by this myself, frankly. But this is *your* fault.

CARLTON. ...motley collection / of dolts and...

*(***SWENSON*** removes his patrol belt, hands it to* **PITTMAN***, who puts it aside.)*

SWENSON. You're arresting a police officer.

PITTMAN. It's awkward for everyone. But you're unreliable, Chief. *(to* **LEE***)* Put him in / the back.

CARLTON. Ignorant, toothless, / inbred...

LEE. / Come on.

PITTMAN. Shut up, Berg.

*(***LEE*** begins moving* **SWENSON*** off to the holding room.)*

SWENSON. You're gonna lock me up in my own jail?

PITTMAN. Sorry. / Shouldn't be long now.

CARLTON. Dumbest bunch of / ignorant, hayseed...

SWENSON. This doesn't stop here! People are gonna hear about this!

*(***LEE*** and* **SWENSON*** exit.)*

*(***PITTMAN***, still wielding the baton, turns to* **CARLTON***.)*

CARLTON. I don't know where she went.

PITTMAN. You know what, buddy? I believe you.

(He approaches him, baton in hand.)

(The fax machine comes to life.)

There's my fax.

CARLTON. Can I ask you something, Pittman?

PITTMAN. No, you really can't.

(He collects the fax. Begins reading it. **LEE*** enters.)*

LEE. Is that the letter?

PITTMAN. Check the email, too.

LEE. Are we killing people?

PITTMAN. Check the email.

*(He reads the letter again, carefully, while **LEE** checks email on his cell.)*

LEE. There's an attachment.

PITTMAN. From Spalding?

LEE. Yeah.

*(**PITTMAN** folds up the letter, puts it in his pocket.)*

Are you gonna let *me* read it? Hello?

*(**PITTMAN** shoots **CARLTON** dead.)*

SWENSON. *(off)* What happened?! What's happening out there?!

PITTMAN. Now let's get an APB out on that chick.
Bob? Snap to it, Bob.

LEE. What?

PITTMAN. Get an APB out on that chick. Let's go.

LEE. I don't know how to do that.

PITTMAN. We'll call Washington. But first, call up her record.

*(**LEE** sits at the computer.)*

LEE. Did he say what her name was?

PITTMAN. I don't know.

LEE. *(calling)* Chief!

PITTMAN. Don't do that. Just look it up.

LEE. Under what? I don't know how to use this software.

PITTMAN. It's gonna b– It'll be analogous to… Let me make this call. You'll figure it out.

(He makes a call on his cell.)

LEE. You know, Dale, she's obviously not an amateur.

PITTMAN. Obviously. So what.

LEE. Someone like her, she'll vanish into thin air. She's probably a million miles from here.

PITTMAN. We're the government. We've got…*(on phone)* Hey, it's me. Let me talk / to…

(*TANYA bursts in through the main door, wielding a hunting rifle.*)

TANYA. Alright, you fuckers! Freeze! Get your fucking hands up! Get 'em up!

(*They do.*)

(*to* **PITTMAN**) Give me your gun, asshole. Take it out.

(**PITTMAN** *takes out his gun, but she can't reach it and keep the rifle level, too.*)

Put it on the desk, stupid.

(*He does.*)

Put down the phone, fuckin' phone monkey.

(**PITTMAN** *puts the phone on the desk.*)

Back up.

(*She picks up* **PITTMAN**'s *gun, points it at them. Lays down the rifle. Yells into the cell phone.*)

Hold the line, motherfuckers, he'll be back in a minute! (*to* **LEE**) You think you're *exempt?* Give me your gun.

(**LEE** *unholsters his gun.* **TANYA** *starts backing* **PITTMAN** *up toward* **LEE**.)

Now, I'm just here to bust Carlton out of this shithole, so just stay calm and…and…

(*She sees* **CARLTON** *on the floor.*)

The fuck, dude? Carlton? Carlton? Are you dead? Is he dead? Did you kill him?

PITTMAN. Listen, miss…

(*She fires wildly at them both.*)

TANYA. FUCKERS!

(**PITTMAN** *dies.* **LEE**, *badly wounded, levels his gun at* **TANYA**. *She walks right up to him and simply takes the gun out of his hand.*)

Fuckers!

SWENSON. *(off)* What's happening out there?

(**TANYA** *screams into the cell phone:*)

TANYA. Motherfuckers! *(She leaps up onto the desk.)*
THIS IS HOW IT STARTS, MOTHERFUCKERS!

(She screams:)

MOTHERFUCKERS!

(…while firing both guns into the air.)

(Blackout.)

(Skynyrd.)